Joseph McGee Private Investigator: Book Two

CROSSING THE CULT

McGee Confronts a Murderous Cult

I0549057

Carl Douglass

Neurosurgeon Turned Author Writes With Gripping Realism

Since 1978

PO Box 221974 Anchorage, Alaska 99522-1974
books@publicationconsultants.com—www.publicationconsultants.com

ISBN 978-1-59433-580-8
eISBN 978-1-59433-581-5
Library of Congress Catalog Card Number: 2015952501

Manufactured in the United States of America.

Dedication

To the people of the wild, Wild West
and a nod to the effete Easterners.

Disclaimer

A ll of the six novellas in the McGee Series are works of fiction and should not be construed as representing real persons, places, or events. Some names of real persons and places appear but only for the purpose of creating a setting in the real world or as a mention of historical circumstances. None of the real people or the real places were actually involved in the fictional portrayals found in these short books. All of the events described were created from the author's imagination.

Chapter One

1881

Petter Arontsen was excommunicated by the Church of Jesus Christ of Latter-day Saints [Mormons] on June 12, 1881 for the most grievous of sins—apostasy. It was his fiftieth birthday, and he never forgot the insult and humiliation inflicted on him by the LDS Prophet. To rub salt in Petter's wound, his excommunication was announced in the church's newspaper, the *Deseret News*, on the day of Petter's fiftieth birthday. Petter lost most of his friends—all of whom were Mormons. At least as important to him was that he also lost most of his business opportunities. His family—four wives and eighteen children—was disillusioned, regarding his expulsion from the church as grossly unfair. They were glad to leave "Zion" and try another place and another life.

The other place was easy. In fact, they moved about following Petter's work opportunities as master mason. He was successful and became anxious to start his own business in a permanent location. That location was an odd one, as it turned out. The family settled in the very middle of Wyoming in a hamlet called Iron Heart in reference to the train locomotives that received scheduled maintenance there. The presence of the trains provided the opportunity Petter needed to make his name and fortune. Iron Heart was located in the center of a shallow depression in the desert floor surrounded by low granite mountains. Petter and his sons established a quarry and attracted highly skilled quarriers. He shipped precisely cut granite blocks around the country and frequently provided master and journeymen masons to supervise the planning and construction of buildings in every major city in America and Lower Canada. By 1910, Petter no longer wielded a hammer and chisel. He made his millions with a pencil and a telegraph.

Iron Heart would have remained a hamlet housing skilled quarriers, masons, shippers, salesmen, and accountants were it not for the burning need Petter Arontsen had to enlarge the religious universe of those around him. In 1888, he actually purchased the town—lock, stock, and barrel. He became the mayor, primary employer, greatest benefactor, and eventually, the city's major religious figure—almost the only one. He groomed his eleven sons to follow his lead, and together they began to attract followers to Iron Heart—not for work—but to join Arontsen's innovative church that he named—with a modicum of immodesty—The Only True Church of Christ.

Being the home of a church with such a provocative name surely needed the city to change with the times and circumstances. The mayor and the city council—consisting of four of his sons, two daughters, and two sons-in-law, who were all also prominent in the church—voted unanimously to change Iron Heart to The Heart of Eden. By 1900, there was a serious draw from America and soon thereafter from

Eastern and Western Europe, Australia, and New Zealand to The Heart of Eden. Prophet Petter Arontsen—as he became affectionately known—developed a proselytizing network par excellence. The advantages of The Only True Church were many and were extremely appealing: earthly wealth afforded by lucrative work in a well-established industry, polygamy that attracted rich men who could afford to take wives from among the many nubile girls in The Heart of Eden and from around the world, whose passage and promise of a good life was assured by the simple expedient of joining the wealthy congregation.

By the time the Prophet Petter died in 1932, there were 200,000 citizens/members in The Heart of Eden with an average income of $83,000 for a family of four—a small family—and $142,000 for a family of fourteen—more nearly the average. By the standards of the time—the depths of the Great Depression—that was princely. He was wise in almost every respect by maintaining control of almost all aspects of his and his family's lives and the lives of his congregants. He established a hierarchal order that assured a smooth succession in leadership of the church, the city, and the burgeoning businesses based on nepotism.

The Prophet hit upon another highly effective way to ensure tranquility and contentment among the members. The church and the city passed laws that required every member to divest himself and his family of all holdings in return for a guaranteed cradle-to-grave comfortable life. That was highly appealing to the people living on the brink of disaster during the Depression. The other element of control which guaranteed social contentment was that all marriages were controlled by a central "Sacred Marriage Bureau." Members trained in sociology and psychology investigated the compatibility of marital arrangements and granted licenses to those of a marriageable age and with an appropriate work ethic. The system worked, much as society works in Scandinavia—no one stood out; everyone was average; and there was no need for contention and rivalry for jobs or to find a suitable mate.

The next four presidents of the church were selected by the Council of the Prophets—six men handpicked by the president, who were of irreproachable moral character and proven financial ability and stability—all of whom were sons of Petter Arontsen. The next three were grandsons of the founding Prophet. All of the presidents were excellent husbandmen of the large fortune they inherited. Each man was richer than the last; and by 2013, Prophet/President Erasmus Jessen—the first man not directly related to the Arontsen family—had an estate that made him a double billionaire. His three predecessors were also fine managers and were able to pass on an increase of more than a billion dollars.

The liberal policies of The Only True Church adapted with the times and were inclusive rather than exclusive. It was more than social liberalism; it was financially practical because the church attracted people with money who were of both genders, all races, and all sexual persuasions. Some of the less pious sang irreverent songs of praise for the church and its Prophet—the favorite being, "Oh, how the money rolls in, rolls in; oh, how the money rolls in."

It was not until the fall of 2013 that the first fissures began to appear in the idyllic church, town, industry, and social structure in the form of a whistle blower named Devon Carlisle.

Chapter Two

2013

Devon Michael Carlisle joins The Only True Church of Christ in 2001 when he is fifteen years old. The Harold and Martha Carlisle family has four children when they join and four more enter the world in Heart of Eden after they settle into Stephen Randolph Arontsen's community. Harold and Martha divest themselves of three million dollars in investments and savings in a single gift to the church when they leave New York City and move to the middle of wind-swept and barren Wyoming. Following the instructions of the prophet, Harold continues in his financial management business via the internet and is able to work from the family's new location. The family continues to contribute more than a million dollars a year to the church.

Devon graduates from True Church Preparatory School as its valedictorian in 2003 and goes on to the land-grant University of Wyoming in Laramie—more accurately in the high Laramie Plains between the city and the Snowy

Mountain range. There, he follows the prophet's directions and graduates magna cum laude with a BA in business administration and a minor in finance. In 2010, he obtains a masters degree in finance, and a CPA. The costs of all of that education are underwritten by The Only True Church of Christ higher education foundation.

The funding for education comes with strings attached. Each student is obligated to sign a binding contract to work in Heart of Eden or for the church in a location selected by the Council of the Prophets for at least ten years. That is no burden for the second son of the Carlisle family because Devon is a true believer. Devon has a head for numbers and an insight into investment and finance that makes him a serious asset for Prophet/President Arontsen who wants a foothold for the church in the New York Stock market and with the Big Apple's financial giants. Five months before the Prophet's death, he is able to get Devon a seat on the NYSE when a vacancy appears, and a mid-level job as assistant to the CFO of BB&H [Berkeley, Bradley, and Hawthorne], one of the largest and most active of New York's financial houses.

Devon cements his position with BB&H when, in 2011, he is able to expose an embezzlement scheme involving three vice presidents of the company and to provide the evidence used in court to convict them. Devon learns that his true gift is research—to find the nugget or the crime hidden in the mass of numbers and transactions. During that incident, he first came to know McGee & Associates Investigations and to become more than a nodding acquaintance of J.P.A.M.J. McGee, the charismatic and brilliant head of the private investigation company which serves the rich and famous, and even the government, upon occasion.

Devon's entire salary and bonus package is banked directly into the Only True Church of Christ Bank in Heart of Eden,

Wyoming, where other financial geniuses determine where investments are to be made. Devon is granted $80,000 a year plus expenses to maintain his life in New York and Heart of Eden. The new prophet, Erasmus Jessen, agrees with his predecessor that young Devon is an asset and rewards him with the right to marry when he is only twenty-three years old, five years earlier than usual for the tightly controlled religious community. He is even promised that he will be accepted into the Council of the Providers—the support group of five-hundred successful men and women who provide the detail work and the bulk of the income for the Council of the Prophets—and will be granted the special dispensation of beginning his plural marriage life earlier than his peers. It is evident that young Devon Carlisle is being groomed to be one of the Council of the Prophets when a vacancy occurs.

2013 is the beginning of a major life change for Devon, his family, and The Only True Church of Christ. That is the year when fissures of doubt appear in the foundation of Devon's faith. From early childhood, Devon develops an inquisitive mind coupled with a desire to dig into the roots of the truth. Until 2013, it has not occurred to him to apply those cognitive traits to his church. He probably would never have probed beneath the establishment of the obviously rock-solid financial and then the social structure of the religion for which he testifies fervently in Sunday testifying and glorifying meetings ever since he and his family joined the charismatic brother and sisterhood of believers, had he not stumbled onto an anomaly.

It is a matter of having too much knowledge—not a rare cause of the downfall of intensely devoted religious adherents—and having that knowledge turn up a revelation of sorts. Devon is seeking ways to increase the income of the church; so, he begins a foundation-level study of how the highly successful religious organization functions financially. It takes some digging; but while studying stock market transactions seeking patterns of investing, he finds a disturbing pattern. Hidden in the reams of numbers and stock transaction records is a recurring leitmotif of what Devon knows are greenmail purchases and sales. The Only True Church of Christ has a regular practice of buying a large amount of a company's stock at an inflated price so that the management—fearing a takeover—will be forced to buy it back at an even higher premium to avoid a hostile takeover. The practice is considered unethical by most traders, and the church's transactions are obfuscated by use of dummy trusts and cut-out corporations. The names listed in the companies are rank-and-file church members with no business interest, experience, or involvement.

Then he begins an investigation into whether or not the church has practiced—either intentionally or unintentionally—inappropriate or even illegal short sale transactions. What he learns in that effort convinces him that he is in over his head, and he decides to contact McGee & Associates Investigations for professional help.

Chapter Three

2013

McGee's private office line phone rings, waking him from a reverie that features fly-fishing on the Provo River in Utah, one of his favorite getaways and mind cleansers.

"Hello," he says.

"Mr. McGee, thank you for taking my call. You probably don't remember me, but I'm Devon Carlisle from the Berkeley, Bradley, and Hawthorne financial firm. Maybe you'll remember that you and I worked on an embezzlement issue involving three vice presidents of the company, which worked out well for BB&H and me."

"I do remember. How are you doing lately, Devon?"

"I'm fine personally, but I have a delicate problem."

"You've reached the delicate investigations department. Tell me what's going on?"

McGee presumes that he is about to hear some personal problem that Devon needs to hide. He remembers how strict the young man is about his religion and knows that a personal peccadillo would be a mountain where for others it would be a molehill. He is surprised by Devon's answer.

"It's not really about me. It's about the church, or at least somebody who controls money for the church. It would be very destructive if it ever got out. In a nutshell, I am still an assistant to the CFO of BB&H, and I handle the church's investment accounts. I have found evidence of greenmail offenses and maybe even some short sale transactions that are not altogether ... what shall I say ... kosher."

"I'm aware of your expertise. How can McGee Investigations help?"

"I want a very private and very complete forensic accounting of the transactions by the church; and I want it to be kept a secret until all of the evidence is available; so, I don't go off half-cocked and injure the church and destroy myself and my family."

"With regards to secrecy, how would you pay for our services, Devon?"

"I thought of that problem. Before I called you, I set up a company which I call BB&H Educational Services using my wife's maiden name as the president and CEO. I have very considerable discretion over business expenditures for the church investments, and I can bill that account without the fact being known that I am the one looking into the accounts. So, that's not the problem. What is a more likely concern is that anything I do within the company will be tracked by IT and security. Can you hack into the account and check it out surreptitiously?"

"Probably, but we will be in a grey area legally. In the end, if or when any of this becomes public, you will have to be the guy whose name appears, not mine. Agreed?"

"Yes. I am looking at the future, and it looks like this might become a real problem. But I just cannot turn a blind eye. That would be dishonest, and I can't live with that."

"Is it your intent to be a whistleblower, Devon?"

"Gosh, I hope not. I would like to have all of the data and be able to present it to the Prophet/President and the Council of Prophets; so, it can be corrected. I am afraid there is a rotten apple in the barrel somewhere, and they need to know who it is. So far as I can tell by my limited research thus far, we are talking millions, maybe even billions, if this all goes back for decades like I'm afraid it does."

"All right, Devon. First, I think we should not communicate by regular phones again; and we should not meet in my offices or yours. Go out and buy a box of burner phones. Pay cash and program my private number into a few of them. Change phones every month at least. Second, you will need to meet with my partner, Caitlin O'Brian, who is a top-flight analyst with a lot of experience in stock transactions and chicanery. She used to be a NYPD detective."

"Oh, Mr. McGee, I certainly don't want to get the police involved."

"Caitlin is very sensitive to the distinctions between private and police investigations. No police until and unless you want to. We contract to give you the best evidence we can produce, and you can deal with what you learn at your discretion. And, just call me McGee. Everybody does. Okay if we all call you Devon?"

"Sure."

"So, meet me tomorrow in Lederman's Grill on fifth. I'll bring Caitlin and get you two together; so, we can get this show on the road."

"Good, and thank you … McGee. I wish I could just ignore this, but sometime this will blow up if serious changes aren't made. I am hoping to get in head of the problems.

Devon is sitting in a back booth when Caitlin comes into the restaurant. McGee gave her a good description of the young man; so, she is able to pick him out in a couple of minutes. Both of them are strictly punctual and no-nonsense workers; so, they take to each other immediately.

"Devon, I presume?" Caitlin says.

"And you're Caitlin, I presume?" he says.

"I am."

She slides into the booth, facing him.

"Have you eaten here before?" she asks.

"Never. Is it any good? I'm starving."

"They make a mean burger and a great pastrami on rye."

"Pastrami sounds great. What'll you have?"

"I have to watch my girlish figure; so, I have to choke down another salad."

They laugh and eat their lunches before getting down to business.

Passing on dessert, Caitlin begins the business conversation while Devon has a sorbet combo.

"I got the general idea from McGee about what's going on. Do you have records with you to get my accounting people going?"

"I didn't think it would be safe; so, I brought a thumb drive. I can tell you that it's not complete, and there is still plenty of work to do. Here."

He looks around to be sure they are not being watched and slides the USB device and a burner phone under the table to her.

She nods and slips the two items into her jacket pocket.

"I'll get back to you. May take a couple of days. Have your burner with you all the time—okay?"

"I will. Have a nice day."

Caitlin and her executive assistant, Rosalie Hertel, and David Harger, the IT officer for McGee & Associates, and his two brilliant nerds start on the project as soon as she gets back to the office.

David hacks into the BBH investment accounts with such ease that it would be frightening to their religious young client if he knew the details.

Once he is in, he asks Caitlin, "Where should we start?"

"Since greenmail is a practice that mainly involves mergers and acquisitions, we should probably start there."

"I agree," she says, and four computers begin to buzz.

Greenmail is named for blackmail and in the stock investment form of blackmail, money gets paid to an aggressor—The Only True Church of Christ, in this instance—by the victim corporation to halt acts of aggression being perpetrated against it. The accounting reveals very early on that the church has no intention of taking over other corporations on any wholesale basis. In fact, the McGee investigators only find four instances of actual takeover, and none of them were profitable. In the other two hundred eighty-six aggressive takeover attempts, the church—as corporate raider—yielded to the corporations, which retained control of their companies. On average, the church obtained greenmail payments—after all sales were finalized—of sixty-four million dollars, with a low of twenty-two million and a high of one hundred forty-six million dollars going into the investment accounts of The Only True Church of Christ annually. The investigators spend five full business days accumulating the evidence and compile it into a thick printout book and save the damning data on three thumb drives—two for Devon Carlisle and one for McGee & Associates.

Richard Crenshaw asks the obvious question, "This has got to be illegal, is this not? Maybe we need to get our lawyers involved to protect ourselves and to give needed information to the client."

"I'll get Nichols and Anderton on it. We use them pretty frequently on questions of legality when it comes to stock manipulation. Remember the Russian short sale attack on the stock exchanges a while back? We used them to gather the evidence. I am all in favor of the CYA approach of getting the lawyers involved," Caitlin says.

The following week, Devon joins Caitlin and Harger from McGee's and Tom Anderton from the law firm for the legal aspects of what they have been working on. For security, they meet in Anderton's office conference room. He has a laptop projection of a PowerPoint program of the pertinent legal points already up on the conference room screen when the others arrive.

They all introduce themselves and get immediately down to the findings.

Tom says, "You have found multiple legal irregularities. Some of the greenmail material is in a legal grey area and some is clearly illegal. All of the short sales are outright illegal, and they have been very artfully obfuscated in a mountain of data. I don't know how long it would have been before all of this was discovered if Devon had not looked into it. That was good work, Devon."

Devon nods in acknowledgment but is none too enthusiastic about where all of this is headed.

"So, a little legal tutorial for all of us. Let's start with the greenmail issues with some history.

"*Paying* greenmail became controversial in the eighties. Long before that, stock market critics viewed it as harmful to U.S. business interests and wanted it to be made criminal; but the courts were slow to act. The critics argued that greenmail is little more than a bribe, and bribes in the stock market are illegal. What produced progress was the litigation instituted by corporate shareholders. They protested the obvious: greenmail during takeover bids is frequently just a means of extorting profits. It wasn't until well into the nineties that state legislatures began to take an interest. One of the examples—taught in law schools—is when a famous corporate raider used greenmail to try and take over Disney in 1984. He bought nearly six and a half percent of Disney stock before the corporation execs caught on. They almost immediately announced a nearly $400 million acquisition of their own stock to make the company less attractive and that stopped the takeover. The corporate raider gracefully accepted that he had failed and cried all the way to the bank to deposit his nearly $60 million profit.

"Of course, that was a very expensive alternative for the Disney board, even with their vast resources. Then the stockholders weighed in. Later that same year, the stockholders sued the directors of the corporation and the corporate raider and won an injunction—one of the very few judgments which pointed the legal finger at greenmail practices themselves as constituting unjust enrichment. The poor raider had to return all but about twenty million dollars. Strange as it may seem, he was not all that upset at losing the suit. Disney got a wrist slap and had to promise not to do it again. There were those who charged that Disney's caving in to greenmail was the equivalent of embezzlement by the directors and out-and-out blackmail by the corporate raiders.

"Other states—including Ohio and Pennsylvania—came to view greenmail the same way the Disney judge did and passed stringent laws which required corporate raiders to return all of their greenmail profits. You may be surprised to learn that there are doubts about the constitutionality of such laws, and the issue has stagnated. The question of legality of greenmail remains far from settled."

"Caitlin and David and their people have found some pretty clear-cut instances of short sales which were never properly dealt with and stockholders and corporations took it in the shorts without any comeuppance so far. Can you tell us where we are with what has been learned about shorting by the church?" Devon asks.

"Another tutorial is in order," the attorney says. "First, a little lawyerly disclaimer. The evidence is incomplete with only a few days of work into the issues, and the legal requirements to prove illegality on the part of the SEC are quite complicated and stringent. With that caveat, here goes...

"Short sales are legal, and short sellers are allowed to profit from price declines by replacing borrowed securities at a lower price. They are not allowed to profit from insider information. SEC rules are written to ensure that trades settle promptly, thereby reducing settlement failures. There is an SEC regulation called SHO which has quite tight requirements for short sales of borrowed securities. SHO requires short sellers who fail to deliver securities after the legal and contractual settlement date to close out their position immediately. The exception to the SHO rule is for sellers who qualify as bona fide market makers for a limited amount of extra time to close out—and none of the presently investigated short sales appear to qualify.

"My assistants and I have had the new SEC OCIE [Office of Compliance Inspections and Examinations] Risk Alerts reg books open to be sure that any and all of the trades we are studying do not constitute options trading that circumvent SEC short sale rules. From your work and ours, we found seventy-seven instances over the past twenty years of options trading that seemed to have been executed for that very purpose, which is illegal. Many only gave the *impression* of satisfying the OCIE SHO close out requirement. These suspect trades—in my opinion, in effect by evading the rules—are sham close-outs. The only reason I can see that they did not come to the attention of the NYSE MSD [Market Surveillance Division] agents of the exchange and the NYSE Regulation's Enforcement Division is that they were so cleverly spaced over the decades with only a few a year, and none of them reaping huge profits by themselves. However, accumulatively, the profits garnered by The Only True Church of Christ totaled somewhere north of $3 billion. It isn't my responsibility to report these crimes; but, in my opinion, someone should let the NYSE and the SEC see this evidence. I am pretty sure that the Regulations Enforcement Division and the FBI would take a serious interest.

"There are some really worrisome ones that have been buried over the years, including truly abusive naked short sales—out-and-out securities fraud in which stocks were sold without ever being borrowed and without any apparent effort to borrow on the part of the church or its surrogates. We see quite a few short-and-distort false information to drive down stock prices artificially, with fairly large losses by some of the Forbes 500 and DOW-leading companies getting bilked.

"Sometimes, serious attackers create misinformation that looks superficially like intra-company communications that hint at a severe bear market for their stocks because of expected failing year-end mandatory reports. I'm not sure we can prove that the church and its surrogates really did that. If it were true, we would be looking at serious and pretty widespread insider trading. If the church has been responsible for what amounts to an advertising whisper campaign which proves to be false, it is a felony with multiple counts.

"There are some rather obvious instances of trading exclusively in hard-to-borrow securities and threshold list securities; some trading in near-term listed options on such securities, and some large short positions in hard-to-borrow securities or threshold list securities. Only a few of the transactions amount to large failures to deliver positions in accounts, and most of them involve multiple securities. At last count we have identified at least sixty-two counts of continuous failure to deliver positions, a few counts of using buy-writes, married puts, deep in-the-money buy-writes or married puts, to satisfy falsely the close-out requirement. Our internet investigations at the law firm have revealed a regular practice of internet "pump and dump" schemes, trading in customizable FLEX options in hard-to-borrow securities and/or threshold list securities—including more than a few with very short-term FLEX options. We can identify collusion among traders to make trades only to take advantage of the option mispricing. Many of the names are outright phonies, and that should have been a red-flag raiser.

"I know that a lot of this is pretty arcane, but the long and the short of it is that several somebodies working for—or in cahoots with—the church are running a long-standing criminal enterprise; and that is the most important set of crimes because it allows the government to raise RICO statute issues and to seek up to life sentences for people involved in the ongoing criminal conspiracy. It's up to you what you do with the information you have, but our advice is that you distance yourselves from that very rich church as far as you can and as soon as you can."

Devon Carlisle feels as if he has been poleaxed and feels very sick. His spiritual, moral, ethical, and social core is under attack. Everything he has believed in since adolescence is crumbling away. With the attack on his faith, for the first time in his short but clear-cut life, he is at a loss for what to do.

Chapter Four

2015

Devon's conscience shifted from hot indignation, to deep sympathy, to a sort of drifting ennui for his church and for his belief in the church. For the better part of two years he vacillates. At times—as he delves into the church's accounts at BB&H—he takes the stance that his beloved Prophet, the Council of Prophets, and the ardently faithful believers in Heart of Eden and around the world are the victims of some nefarious criminal conspiracy. At other—more sober times—he is beset with the niggling notion that the church's leaders are, in fact, the perpetrators; and he strives to keep such thoughts at bay. Most of the time he goes about his work in a minor mental fog, unable to decide what to do.

No decision affords real release from his tension or a satisfactory solution: on the one hand, if he reports his findings to the SEC and the FBI as a good citizen of the United States should, he will bring shame and unwanted negative attention on his family, the holy leaders of Christ's true church, and destruction of all he holds sacred. On the other hand, if he lets things slide—and they are getting demonstrably worse—who is he? What is he?

Devon is not so befogged by indecision that he is almost entirely inert. Literally the day after the fateful meeting with attorney Tom Anderton, Devon chooses a cautious wait-and-see course. He begins diverting some of his own funds on a regular basis into stocks and bonds with the help of a friend, Lindon Wright, a vice president of Merrill Lynch. An investment genius, Wright steers Devon on into a highly successful set of stock investments that take advantage of the increasing stock market indicators following the 2008 Great Recession. By 2015, Devon's holdings have quietly increased to two million dollars in stocks and another million in REITs [Real Estate Investment Trusts]. He knows he needs the cushion, but exactly for what he is unsure.

Events of early 2015 decide the matter for him. In that year, his father is called to fill the vacancy on the Council of Prophets when the elderly Winston Cartwright dies. Since joining The Only True Church of Christ in 2001, that honor is the crowning achievement of his otherwise humble life. Harold has done everything right and has been rewarded handsomely for his piety. His income has risen to $145,000 per year; the church moves him into a home twice the size of the one he and Martha and the four children have occupied since 2001; and, most importantly, he has taken on three more wives—a singular largesse from the church fathers. The Harold Carlisle nuclear family now numbers eighteen, and his extended family—including sons and daughters-in-law and grandchildren—numbers twenty-five.

Of all of those close family members, the one Devon loves the most outside his wife, Katrina, is Ruth Miriam—his youngest sister, named for two Old Testament heroines. In 2015 Ruth turns thirteen. Becoming an adolescent creates problems for Ruth and eventually for the entire family. By some near-miracle of hormones or genetics, Ruth goes from a skinny, gangly, awkward child into a remarkably beautiful and physically mature teenager almost overnight, it seems to the family. She is still an innocent, giggly, vivacious, and difficult thirteen-year-old; but she now has the body of a voluptuous Mediterranean goddess and the face of an angel. Her peers suffer with pimples and painful shyness. Ruth has clear, almost translucent white skin. She has lustrous curly black hair that shines with highlights. The youthful child/woman turns heads wherever she goes.

One of the heads she turns—unbeknownst to her—is that of Prophet Elias Hiram Richland, age sixty-eight. He is the financial director of the church, and the husband of four wives. Richland determines to make Ruth Miriam Carlisle his fifth—and, by far, the youngest—wife. Prophet Richland goes about his courtship quest in all of the correct ways. First, he seeks the permission of Prophet/President Erasmus Jessen who is quick to grant the privilege because Elias Richland is a miracle worker who regularly brings in wealth beyond the dreams of the Prophet/President when he first assumed the mantle of God's true representative on earth. He would have been happy to grant his financial counselor almost anything because Prophet Richland achieves his economic miracles without Jessen ever having to bother with the arcane details of the process.

Second, Richland obtains the permission to take on another wife from his first wife, Rebecca. That is only a pro forma requirement, since Elias is the patriarch and Rebecca only a wife. Obtaining permission from the other wives is not necessary. Third, he approaches Harold Carlisle—his co-prophet on the council—and asks for his blessing. He knows that Harold could harbor doubts about such a union for his beloved daughter; so, he sweetens the pot with the offer of interceding with the Prophet/President to grant Harold the right to take a new, younger wife as well. Harold has no real choice since he is junior to Elias on the council; and he gives in, albeit with some reluctance. Finally, in June when all permissions are in order and Ruth Miriam is three months past her thirteenth birthday; Elias Hiram Richland, age sixty-eight—august member of the church's highest governing body—approaches beautiful and virginal early teenager Ruth Miriam Carlisle.

The approach takes place after Sunday testifying and glorifying services.

Ruth makes it easy and emboldens the older man. She flashes him a sunny smile as she does to everyone else she greets during the exodus from the chapel. He knows she has given him a personal signal.

"My dear," he says, "how lovely you look today."

"Oh, thank you," the guileless girl responds and begins to float away into the crowd.

He stops her with a gentle touch on her bare arm that she hardly notices but which enlivens him.

"Ruth... isn't it?"

"Yes, sir," she says with a mildly quizzical look on her face.

"Oh, don't call me 'sir,' please, just call me 'brother,' or maybe even 'Elias' which is my first name."

Now, he really is being bold, and the girl is aware that this is more than just a casual encounter. Her antennae go up.

What is going on? she wonders to herself.

He smiles broadly.

"I would like to have a word with you... in private, if we could?"

She crinkles her brow, but minding her manners, says, "I suppose that would be all right. When would you like to have a talk? Where?"

This is the moment of truth for Elias. He summons courage.

"Perhaps we could get an ice cream and have our chat. It would not be right to do that on the Sabbath, but how about tomorrow noon?"

Ruth is becoming uncomfortable, and she is alert to possibilities.

"I think that would be okay. Shall we meet in front of Jeff's?"

"I know the place. I understand all the young people like Brother Jeff's ice cream parlor. That would be fine. I will see you then."

They separate and both see the questions on the faces of members of the congregation around them. He is secretly amused and flattered about the implications, and she is secretly worried about what she is getting herself into.

Ruth is a bright girl, and she is sure that her father has given permission for the older man to approach her. Her first thought is to call her brother, Devon, in New York to get his take on the situation; but she decides to hold off until she finds out for sure what the elderly man wants.

Prophet Richland is not at all used to being refused. He has real power in the church and civic community, and uses that power to his advantage on a regular basis. In his mind, he has already sowed the seeds of a successful courtship, and there is no need to be obtuse about his intentions.

He is anxious to finish his vanilla cone; so, he can tell the girl what the rest of her life will be. She is just anxious.

"It is very nice here, and I am enjoying your sweet company. The Lord has come to me and instructed me to tell you of a great blessing he has in store for you."

He gives her a more than avuncular smile.

Her attention is now riveted on him.

"Yes," he says and stammers slightly, which annoys him. "I have been called of the Lord to tell you that you have found favor in His eyes, and that you and I are to enter into the holy covenant of marriage. I have brought you a ring to seal our courtship."

Relieved that the tension of indecision and awkwardness are over, he beams at the lucky girl, waiting for her exulting response. Inwardly, he hopes she will not create a scene with her enthusiasm; but she is only a girl; and he will have to put up with it.

He sees that the magnitude of his offer has overwhelmed the inexperienced and unworldly girl. She stares at the ring in disbelief—not quite the wonderment he is expecting. She looks up into his grey-bearded face with an unspoken question, and he realizes that she is too thrilled to speak. He gives her time. He is a patient man.

"I ... I ... don't understand," is all she can muster. "What does this mean?"

"My dear, child, we are to be married. You will be the wife of one of the prophets. Your future is secured, and heaven will be your reward!"

It is a thrill to him—for all of his earthly power and spiritual experience and influence—to see that he is having such a profound impact on the young girl. It is beyond his highest expectations and arouses him more than anything else has done in a decade.

Girls are unpredictable, he knows that. But what she does next is perplexing. She starts to cry.

Chapter Five

The following day, Devon makes a small but telling discovery while sitting at his computer reviewing recent investment transactions by The Only True Church of Christ through the managers at Berkeley, Bradley, and Hawthorne. For the first time, he encounters a name he recognizes. One of the investments—a legal one—is ordered by a holding company called Hearst Brothers Trust and signed for by its CFO, Elias Hiram Richland. Devon knows Richland. When his father Harold Carlisle was inducted into the Council of Prophets of the church, Richland made an effort to impress upon both Devon and his father that he is the second in line to the president and will be the successor to the ailing Prophet/President. The fact that the Prophet signed the purchase order is not so remarkable, but it is the first time Devon has seen a name on the investment purchase and sales other than the Prophet/President. It occurs to him that he may have just found a small crack in the wall of secrecy of the financial dealings of The Only True Church. That is interesting and will bear watching, Devon thinks, but being too busy at the moment to do anything more about it, he puts the information on a back burner of his mind.

Devon considers himself to be an objective and a thinking man not governed by emotions until he receives a disturbing telephone call from Heart of Eden an hour later. He recognizes the caller ID—it is from home.

"Hi, Mom? Dad? What's up?"

A quavering voice answers, "It's just only me, Devon. It's Ruth."

"Hi, little sister. Something's wrong. What is it?"

She starts to cry, and he lets her gain control on her own.

"Oh, Devon! Something very scary just happened. I mean, it happened yesterday."

"What?"

"You know Prophet Richland...of course you do. That's silly. Anyway, he did the strangest thing yesterday at noon. On Sunday, he asked me to go with him to get an ice cream and to have a talk. I could have been knocked over by a feather. He tried to give me a diamond ring, and he told me that the two of us were supposed to be married—Prophet Richland and me. I'm thirteen...he wants me to be his wife and to get married right away. I don't know what to do. I'm just a kid. I guess I don't look like it, but I am certainly not a grown-up. I'm scared of boys. I've never even held hands or kissed any male except Daddy and you. Help me!"

Devon is dumbfounded. The mention of Richland's name rings a church and a business bell in his mind, and he now cannot get the man's name or image out of his head. He takes a minute to think—to try and think.

"Are you still there?" Ruth asks.

"I am. I hardly know what to think. What did you tell him?"

"I guess I said something like I needed to think. I know he thinks it is a great honor; but all I can think is that he is old;

he has four other wives; he is a grandfather. I know if I refuse to marry him I might even be forced. It has happened, you know. It will hurt Daddy terribly if I make Prophet Richland mad. I want to get educated, see something of the world, have some fun, have boyfriends. Tell me what to do."

Devon is angry. For the first time in his life he has to face the truth about what the church calls "our peculiar institution" and "God's own form of marriage which will be the way in heaven." He has always harbored doubts, especially since moving to New York to work; polygamy is not considered cool there—to say the least. He has been a defender, but that was when it did not hit him in his own gut. His mother has always been unhappy with polygamy, but puts up with it; so, her husband can get ahead in the church and the community. She has never spoken ill of it. But today, Devon Michael Carlisle realizes that he finds the very idea of his innocent little sister being courted by that unpleasant old man—let alone being prodded into a marriage she fears—repugnant and just plain unacceptable.

Devon has been sitting on the horns of a dilemma regarding the financial improprieties he knows about. This call from Ruth is the clincher. Something has to change, and today is the day to do it.

"Look, Ruth. Just lay low and do nothing. I am not going to let you be forced into marriage. I will protect you and look after you no matter what. I'll call Dad and Mother. Then I am going to fly to Laramie and rent a car and drive to Heart of Eden. I have needed to talk to the council for almost two years now. I guess you make it urgent. Keep out of his way and wait for me."

"Thank you, big brother. I knew you would know what to do."

As soon as Ruth hangs up, Devon calls his father.

"Dad, we have a problem."

"What is it, son?" Harold asks, alerted and maybe mildly alarmed.

"We actually have two problems. The first is that Prophet Richland asked our little Ruth to marry him. She's an innocent thirteen-year-old, and she absolutely wants nothing to do with marriage to anyone now, and most certainly not to a man old enough to be her grandfather…."

Harold starts to interrupt, but Devon pushes on, "Dad, I cannot believe that you gave your approval. What were you thinking?"

"Listen, young man, think who you are talking to. To answer your question, I was thinking of Ruth's and our family's future. That includes you and me, boy. What are *you* thinking?"

"Dad, it pains me to hear you say that. It is time for our whole family to step back and look at this objectively."

"You have been corrupted by the world, Devon. I am beginning to fear for your very soul. Come to your senses, son, before it's too late."

"It's already too late, I guess, Dad. There is something even more important. I need to talk to the Prophet/President and the Council of Prophets in an emergency meeting this very day. I will be in Heart of Eden by five o'clock. Please arrange for me to communicate with them all. I have something that is important to the security and future of the church. It is time for them to learn what I know."

"Good heavens, Devon! What is it?"

"I don't want to say anything to anyone before I can present all of the evidence I have collected. Please do this one thing for me."

"All right, Devon, but I have a strong feeling that I and the family are going to regret this day for the rest of our lives. Change and challenge come hard in this church, and you had better tread lightly."

Devon thinks about calling Prophet Richland; but, upon reflection, he decides it is the better part of wisdom to make his presentation to the council before there is any direct contact between himself and Richland.

He calls Caitlin O'Brian instead.

"Hello," Caitlin says.

"Hi, Caitlin. This is Devon Carlisle. I presume that you got the last two thumb drives?"

"I did. They're in the safe."

"Good. Sorry, but I don't have time to talk. I need something in a hurry."

"Anything. What do you need?"

"I need to bug a conference room in Heart of Eden starting today. This is probably the only time I will ever get into that room again. Can you get me something I can just stick to the table, small enough that it won't be seen easily?"

"Got just the thing. In fact, I'll get two of them to you. Are you in your office?"

"For about half an hour."

"That's enough. I'll bring the stuff myself. They have an adhesive and a long-lasting little battery. They will be voice-activated; so, they will probably be useful for months."

"Thanks. See you shortly."

Prophet Richland catches up to Prophet Carlisle as they walk up the path to the chapel door.

"A moment before we go in. I have a couple of quick things we need to talk about. I'll get right to the point: I am confused and don't know how to take your Ruth's reaction to my proposal. I need you to have a talk with her. She needs to learn obedience apparently."

Harold Carlisle bristles at the effrontery of the man giving him orders on how to deal with his child, but he keeps a bland face and listens.

"And, tell me what is it that your boy is up to? Seems pretty irregular for a young man with no real authority to be demanding an emergency meeting of the council—of his betters."

That line of conversation does not sit particularly well, either; but Harold answers as calmly as he can, "I have no idea. However, Devon has a very cool head and is not given to rashness. I think it is likely that what is going to be presented is important and that it is about money. We'll just have to wait and see."

Devon is waiting outside the chapel's conference room door at five to five—ever the punctilious one. He greets each Prophet and the secretary as they file in and take their seats. Only his father and Prophet Richland avoid the handshake.

Prophet /President Erasmus Jessen opens the meeting.

"Brother Walter, will you give us the invocation?"

Prophet Walter is known for his flowery sermons, and is also known to make his prayers into sermons. This is no exception. He expounds to the Lord—and incidentally to the assembled leaders—incongruously on keeping the Sabbath Day holy.

"Thank you. Now, since you requested this meeting, young Devon, it is time to explain yourself."

"Thank you, President. I have brought copies of research I have conducted during my work at the Berkeley, Bradley, and Hawthorne Company in New York."

He makes something of a flourish with his left hand, pushing the documents towards the middle of the handsome black walnut table. When he is sure that all eyes are on the bound documents, he slips his right hand under the table and attaches the listening device.

"Now, brothers, let me explain what you can study at your leisure when I leave. I will summarize. I am a CPA, and I am entirely able to read and understand business ledgers. In brief, what I found is a long record of financial improprieties either on the part of, or perpetrated against, our church. I am not yet sure which is the case."

"How dare you?" Prophet Richland lashes out, his face red with anger, "I demand that you shut your mouth this instant. This is blasphemy."

The other men in the room seem only to be shocked.

"I was prepared for just such a reaction; so, allow me only a few more sentences, then you all can decide whether it is blasphemy or just uncomfortable truth." He hardly pauses and plunges ahead. "The church, or someone or some group acting in the name of the church, has performed many trans-actions called greenmail and many others which are con-sidered to be outright illegal short sales and embezzlement from companies associated with our many financial arms. Be angry; be hateful; excommunicate me; but you ignore the evidence I bring to you at your peril."

The room is silent. Devon stands up and walks around the table to an empty chair next to his father.

"Dad, I have no desire to embarrass you or the church. You have to believe that, but this information has to come to light among the members of the council."

As he talks earnestly to his father, knowing that glaring eyes are locked on him, he calmly reaches under the table and attaches the second electronic listening device.

Before he exits the room, he makes one last statement, "I am on my way to brief the SEC and the FBI. I suggest that all of you as a group—and anyone who feels personally threatened—get a good lawyer. You are going to need one."

As the door closes behind him, he hears a furor. He is certain that the explosive material he has presented will occupy the men for a long time. He gets into his rental car and drives directly to the family home. On the way, he calls Ruth on his burner phone and tells her to pack quickly for an extended trip. She is shocked but resigned, having decided to give herself over to her brother whom she trusts.

At the house, Devon quickly explains to his mother what has been going on—the short version—and gives her a burner phone in which he has downloaded the number of his own expendable cell phone.

"Hide it and only use it to call me. Your safety depends on that. I am sure of that. I will take care of Ruth. She is not going to marry her grandpa."

Martha Carlisle is not quite sure whether to be relieved, frightened, angry, or resigned. She decides on the latter and bids her children good-bye, perhaps for the last time. She goes into her room and has a good cry.

Chapter Six

That evening, Devon moves his wife and Ruth to a safe house in lower Manhattan arranged by McGee. Caitlin helps them settle in and promises to send some of the office staff around the next day to provide any additional help they might need.

For the first time, Devon meets the very impressive man who will be in charge of all security matters for the young Carlisle family. Ivory White is an unlikely name for the blackest man he has ever seen. Ivory is—in the vernacular—the muscle of the McGee organization. The man is a magnificent specimen—tall, athletic, bald, arrogant, and looks like he can be mean if needs be—and they gather from McGee that is quite often the case in his line of work. Whatever the correct definition of his responsibility is, it is best known by its euphemism—"special investigations." He does all of the personal security for high profile clients. McGee lets it be known that—for all of his martial arts and other physical skill sets—Ivory is extremely intelligent. He is a remarkable linguist who speaks six of the most useful languages of the

800 used by the citizens of the most densely populated city in the country if not the world. He is armed to the teeth.

He makes Devon nervous, but the two women in the family take to him immediately. They feel safe with him, and that is the point of the whole exercise. The following morning, two of Ivory's security agents—one of whom is Ed Rainer, the chauffeur for McGee & Associates—escort him as unobtrusively as possible to his office in BB&H. The door is locked, and his key no longer works. Devon, Hector, and Ed all know the jig is up; but just to humor Devon, they all traipse down to HR to see what is going on. The secretary for Human Relations has a box of Devon's private stuff, and a notice—literally a pink slip—informing him that his services have been terminated. Big surprise. There is no one about who can shed any light on what is happening; and apparently no one cares, since all telephones Devon tries are busy "for the rest of your life," one snotty secretary tells him.

Devon and his bodyguards drive back to the safe house to check on his girls. Caitlin reassures him and moves him out to the limo for a ride to Broadway between Duane and Worth Streets, south of Canal Street and north of City Hall. Ed drops them off at the 26 Federal Plaza building, and Devon and Hector take an elevator ride to the twenty-third floor where the five borough FBI offices are located. In addition to the special agents of the FBI, there are three agents of the SEC—who came over from their Brookfield Place office on Vesey Street—all waiting to meet the whistleblower. Caitlin nods to the agents whom she has already met. Three days ago, she delivered the copious numbers of documents collected by Devon with considerable assistance from hackers at McGee & Associates.

FBI Special Agent Henry Weintrobe extends his hand to Devon, and Caitlin makes introductions all around.

Since they are in the FBI's house, Weintrobe takes the lead—not especially unusual for FBI agents.

"We have had a chance to talk to Ms. O'Brian, Mr. Carlisle; so, we don't need to put you through a lot of questioning. There are several procedural matters to take care of, and we should deal with them right now. I have a couple of questions about your involvement in all of this. When did you discover the irregularities at BB&H?"

Devon takes the question and runs with it in the interest of efficiency. In a few crisp sentences, the FBI and SEC agents know of his membership in The Only True Church of Christ, his employment at BB&H largely for the purpose of handling church accounts, and of his none-too-friendly conference with the Council of Prophets in Heart of Eden, Wyoming.

"I just have to ask: where in the world is Heart of Eden, and how did it get that unlikely name?"

Devon tells them, and the agents and Caitlin just shake their heads.

There are several more questions about the religion—which all of the agents now refer to as a "cult."

"Did you enrich yourself or your family from the ill-gotten gains from Wall Street, Mr. Carlisle?"

"Only to the extent that I set aside an account in another financial institution to protect myself and my family if—or now is a fact—when I am cut off. It hasn't happened yet, but I expect to be excommunicated."

"Is that really a bad thing, given the criminal activities that we are about to investigate?"

"Most definitely for me. The church will take my wife and give her to another man if I don't convince her and protect her. I will have to go to great lengths to protect my sister and—if at all possible—my father, mother, and my other siblings. But I have accepted all of that. Having the FBI and SEC step in has to be viewed as the lesser of evils."

"Well, thanks for the high compliment, Mr. Carlisle," Special Agent Weintrobe says with a friendly smile.

Devon nods in acceptance and resignation.

"Besides," he says, "my family is so dyed-in-the-wool that they will reject me in favor of the church anyway."

It is a sad statement of the truth, and Devon knows it all too well.

"We'll execute search warrants on BB&H and church headquarters in Wyoming today. It wouldn't be a bad idea for you to lay low for a while, Mr. Carlisle. Why don't you and your wife take a little trip with your sister, Ruth. I don't think the nice church folks are murderous, but you never can tell in cases like this," Weintrobe says.

Ed picks up Devon and Caitlin outside the front door of the federal plaza building, and they return to the McGee & Associates offices.

"How did it go?" McGee asks.

"Okay. The die is cast, and there's no turning back now," Devon says. "It is a hard thing to have the world you have known and counted on all your life just crumble around you. I know I shouldn't be upset, but those people are the only real friends I have—and my family. It is going to be a very difficult adjustment."

"I have a suggestion," McGee offers. "Maybe this whole thing is a matter of just a few rotten apples, and the senior church authorities and the rank-and-file will welcome you back and applaud what you have done to straighten things out. And—even if more of them are corrupt than you think right now and they don't accept you back into the fold—you haven't lost any real friends. Remember, in that scenario you are the good guy; and you are on the side of the angels."

"*How come I don't feel so great about it, then?*" Devon muses, mainly to himself.

"Back to business. We don't really know what they're going to do; but to be on the safe side, I want you and Ruth to go with Ivory to a safe location until this blows over. Transfer all of your personal funds to this bank under the name of Riley Sargent. They are expecting the transaction. We've used this place before, and your money will be secure and untraceable there. The arrangements will be rigid: only you and I can withdraw funds. The password for the account is "Safe_HAVEN07-30-15$#." The numbers are today's date. Ivory and his men will drive you back to your apartment; so, you can clear it out. Tell no one—and I mean no one—where you are going or about the bank arrangement. I know you have burner cell phones. Use them exclusively, but try and communicate as much as possible through me or Caitlin, okay?"

Devon nods in agreement.

Chapter Seven

July 30, 2015

Twelve FBI and six SEC special agents march into the offices of Berkeley, Bradley, and Hawthorne in New York, and another ten FBI and six SEC agents enter the offices in the central chapel of The Only True Church of Christ in Heart of Eden, Wyoming, at the same time—11:00 AM in New York, and 9:00 AM in Wyoming. The timing is intended to prevent any communication from either office. The agents present the warrants and—as the first order of business—confiscate all cell phones, computers, and other electronic communications devices, and shut down all landline telephones. Once modern communication silence is achieved, the agents systematically load up all financial records for examination elsewhere and at the convenience of the two federal agencies. The scene in both New York and Wyoming is one of organized confusion, and one FBI agent is tasked to take advantage of that apparent confusion and hyperactivity to plant a dozen listening devices. Officers of BB&H and of the church are detained and taken into custody; those in New York are taken to the main office in Manhattan; and those in Heart of Eden are transported to the regional office on East B Street in Casper.

Custodial guards maintain security in the BB&H investment offices—the entire thirty-third floor of the building—and at the main chapel in Heart of Eden. No one is allowed in or out of either location without FBI sanction. As expected, a mass of attorneys, agents, and persons of interest clog the law enforcement facilities; and a seventy-two-hour marathon of questioning begins. Also—as expected—the personal interviews are largely unproductive. Most of the detainees act on advice from their attorneys and keep silence, and a few plead the protections of the Fifth Amendment of the Constitution. None of this comes as a surprise to the FBI or the SEC since they consider this set of encounters to be preliminary. They are prepared for a lengthy investigation based mostly on what they expect to learn from the voluminous printed and electronic records that have been confiscated. The investigation yields results almost immediately: twenty-two lower-echelon BB&H and church functionaries--acting through their attorneys--accept immunity in return for revealing evidence. The coup for the federal agents is that the CFO of BB&H—who is in the plot up to his eyebrows and knows it—agrees to a plea bargain that permits him to avoid prison.

None of the members of the Council of Prophets speak a word other than to give their names—not even Prophet Harold Carlisle, Devon's father. Since they cannot be held longer without being arrested, and the evidence is not yet sufficient to make arrests; everyone is released with the admonition that they remain available for repeat questioning.

Prophet/President Erasmus Jessen maintains a stolid calm throughout the insulting questions. However, when he returns to Heart of Eden, he vents his fury at two trusted prophets—Elias Hiram Richland, the financial director of the church, and Zachariah Arontsen Bartholomew, the only remaining Arontsen relative on the council; and the man who has received the most money for the longest period of time from the questionable business transactions. The men meet in the house Richland maintains for his docile fourth wife. Unfortunately—for the future of the council—Bartholomew carries a small tape recorder. He is a survivor and has no intention of going down with the ship he perceives to be sinking.

Jessen shouts, "The minions of Satan are about us. I have warned against acceptance of the laws of man and those who enforce them. God is on our side and; with Him, we outnumber our enemies. We are in a fight for our very existence. I had thought the struggle would come upon us because of our peculiar institution as it did for the heretics in Utah, but the Lord has seen fit to have it come upon us from another direction. He will provide our salvation, brethren. We must open our hearts and minds to Him; so, we can know the way. We must contain our anger, but we must act!"

"Prophet/President, allow me to try and find a solution before we consider rash measures. I believe that the traitor, Devon Carlisle, is the key false witness against us. I also believe that he—like Samson of old—has a weakness. Let me see what I can do. I am certain that his young sister wishes to be my wife, and I think she will be able to get through to the errant brother," says Richland.

Jessen calms down, "That may be the answer. We cannot fail; the Lord is counting on us. Do what you have to do. Make this spawn of Satan come to the light of truth. He can come back into our good graces; he can once again be the recipient of our generosity. Or he may have to see reason with stronger persuasion. You remember our problems with the church historian a decade ago, those so-called whistle-blowers that Prophet/President Stephen Randolph Arontsen and you dealt with only five years ago, and the Lefler girl last year. Your work has been invaluable, my friend. I will give you a free hand, but I ask that you keep me informed this time around."

"You can count on me, my prophet and president. I will not fail you, the church, or the Lord," Richland says earnestly.

Neither of the two other prophets take note that Prophet Zachariah Arontsen Bartholomew does not say a word during the intense conversation.

Prophet Richland's first action after leaving his two brother prophets is to seek out Prophet Carlisle at his home. He politely requests the opportunity to talk to Harold and his wife Martha.

Martha invites the senior prophet in, "Is there anything I can get you, your holiness?"

"No, I would just like to have a chat about recent events. I am afraid that there have been some misunderstandings between me and your family. I wish to correct those misunderstandings in the spirit of what Christ would do. Is your husband available?"

"He is. I think he is in his study. I'll get him."

"Thank you."

Harold Carlisle comes to the living room with his wife. It is apparent that he is less than enthusiastic about meeting with Prophet Richland.

"What is it that I can do for you, Senior Prophet?" he asks.

"Ah, my brother, I hope that it is what I can do for you! It seems that we got off on the wrong foot recently on two issues, and I would like to make sure that all is well between us; by that I mean to include you, Martha, your children—including that fine young man, Devon, and his wife."

Martha looks earnestly, almost pleadingly at her husband.

"I am certainly interested in anything you have to say, Senior Prophet."

"Please, while we are in the privacy of your home, and since we are friends, could we just be Elias, Harold, and Martha? It is much warmer that way, don't you think?"

"All right, Elias—Martha and I are comfortable with the informality."

Martha is a good deal more comfortable than her husband, and that fact is not lost on Elias.

"I believe there has been an overreaction on the subject of church finances of late. The council has reconsidered the decision to exclude Devon from his involvement. We are well aware of his contributions, and wish him to resume his work at BB&H. However, we have had difficulty in contacting him. Perhaps you could help."

"Elias, we understand that our son has been excommunicated and cut off from the church and the Lord. How can he function within the faith as an outcast?" Martha asks.

"Oh, my dear, things are not nearly so grim as that! It is true that some heated words were exchanged, and it is also true that the subject of church sanction did come up. However, at my insistence, nothing came of the excommunication conversation. In fact, one of the reasons I came to your home is to admit before you and the Lord that I was hasty; and I wish to have a friendly chat with Devon and to get things back on track. I need your help for that. And while we are at it, you no doubt recall that I have proposed to your splendid daughter, Ruth, and am waiting for an answer to my request that she become my wife. I was quite convinced that she was desirous that we marry, but that she was simply overwhelmed with excitement and joy at the thought of it. Therefore, I would appreciate a mother's help in contacting your children; so, we can develop full harmony."

Most of what the man is saying is lies—both of commission and omission. The important lie is that his presence in the Carlisle home is even better than benign.

"What has come of the investigation by the federal authorities regarding church finances? It is my impression that you, in particular, were most put out at Devon for presenting our records to the FBI and SEC to further their investigation. Is that anger to be set aside as well, Elias?"

"Of course it is, my friend," he lies. "In fact, after a time of sober contemplation and after seeking guidance from our Lord through fasting and prayer, I have come to the conclusion that the church has nothing to fear from the authorities; and Devon should be commended, not criticized, for his good work."

The honey is thick; and Elias nearly chokes on it; but he does a good thespian job at hiding his true feelings of hatred and loathing.

Martha looks longingly at her stern husband and says simply, "Please."

"My dear wife, I have never been able to refuse you anything you truly want, but the fact is I do not have any information about his whereabouts or how to get hold of him for the time being."

"Well, Harold, I am his mother; and I do know how to get hold of him. Leave it to me."

Elias adds, "Please tell him for me that we would like to kill the fatted calf and have a celebration welcoming him back to the fold as something of a hero and not the wayward son that our Lord described in the parable of the lost son as found in Luke 15:11–32. Our boy, Devon, will return in honor, not in the ignominy that the wayward son Jesus described did. You will see that I am sincere, and that I intend to make the Carlisle family happy. I had thought to make it a surprise; but since you will have to make the call, Martha, let me give you this information about the Quail Run Resort in the quaint little hamlet of Annandale. That's where we will hold our retreat this year, and it just so happens that the retreat is reserved there for next week. Please encourage Devon, Katrina, and Ruth to make time to join us there. In that relaxed atmosphere, I can bring all to right with each of them."

Martha sets her jaw, and that is the signal to Harold that there would be no stopping her.

Mother Martha calls Devon with her burner phone, and he answers immediately on his. "Anything wrong, Mother. What's going on?"

"Oh, my dear son! It is the exact opposite of 'anything wrong.' Senior Prophet Richland has come with an apology and an olive branch. I have thought all along that this was a much overblown situation, and I am glad that he has offered us a way for the whole family to come back into the fold in full fellowship. Your father and I are only too happy to accept his offers at face value, and I ask you to do this thing for me. This is what is planned."

Martha tells Devon about the entire conversation with the senior prophet, and enthusiastically encourages Devon and Ruth to meet with Richland in the nonthreatening and peaceful environment of the resort. Devon is highly dubious;

but in the end, he agrees that it could be pleasant and productive. At least in such an atmosphere, it will be safe.

"You are a good son," Martha says at the end of the conversation.

Chapter Eight

The first week in August 2015

Devon selects a new burner phone from his supply, throws his old one away, and calls McGee.

"Hello, Devon," McGee answers, recognizing the burner's unusual numbers.

"Hello, McGee," Devon says. "I have a situation I want to run past you."

He tells McGee all of the details about the proposed meeting with the senior officials of The Only True Church of Christ two days hence.

"I have to say that I am suspicious of Richland's motives, but at least it can be an educational experience. What do you think?"

"I am by nature and vocation always suspicious. I understand your need to patch things up; but I think it is too late for that; and no doubt, they will try to convince you not to cooperate with the feds or to testify. In all probability there will be some carrot and some stick. If you insist on going—and I would much rather that you didn't—I advise all due caution."

"I think it is for the best. I have never wanted a complete rupture with the church. It is my roots, after all. I'll be careful. I'll have to do some persuading to get my sister, Ruth, to agree. She doesn't want to meet with Richland, and she'll be hiding behind my leg like a little girl when she does. However, she has never made a clear-cut and clean break, and that has to be done."

"What was that about, Devon?" Ruth asks when he clicks the call off.

"Things are getting interesting; maybe even hopeful."

Devon repeats the now familiar story of the FBI and SEC investigations, and of the overture made to their father and mother. He makes a point of telling Ruth about the stress their mother is making for them to go to the upstate resort and to give reconciliation a try.

"You and I both know that Mother wants you to accept Senior Prophet Richland's proposal because it will be a big feather in her cap. She just wants the best for you. Romantic love has never been an important theme for either her or Dad."

"You're not going to pressure me, too, are you, Devon? I couldn't stand that. I am not going to marry that man of my own free will, and that's final."

Her face looks like it is final.

"It's completely your decision, little sister. I will have your back all the way."

Martha studies about the area of the resort, its history, and gets directions for getting there. She unobtrusively looks up current resort attire on the internet and has herself a small shopping spree. She and Harold fly first class on Delta to New York's JFK airport and rent a car—a full size Cadillac SUV—something she has never done before. She views this impending experience as a life-changer, and is as excited as a girl as she and Harold drive into the Hudson River Valley.

Coming from the bleak badlands of Wyoming into the natural green beauty of the area of upstate New York that has come to be known as "America's Rhineland" is a real pleasure for Martha and the six children still living at home—Harold has reservations. The entire region has been declared to be a U.S. historical district, and the ambiance takes the couple back to a pristine early time in the history of their country. They follow the directions and take a small gravel road off the main highway and approach the Quail Run resort from the east which reveals the expensive view available only from the house. The main building of the resort is a large old neoclassical five-bay facade estate house with a river and mountain view surrounded by open pastures known in history as "pleasure grounds." A large colonial porch overlooks the river in a pristine setting.

Harold comments that "Elias has certainly chosen well. The place is positively tranquilizing. As he says, it is ideal for privacy, luxury, and a restful time."

The children snoop around to find where the many film stars, political figures, and religious luminaries might have stood when they stayed in Quail Run. Less than an hour passes before the older girls bring a written plan for short trips to Bard College for theater productions and lectures. They settle in as if they were regulars. The meetings are scheduled for the next morning, and the evening is free. They all overeat hamburgers, pizza, French fries, root beer floats, and brownies. They all stay up too late and grouse at not being allowed to hit the snooze button on their radio alarms the next day.

It takes some arranging for Devon and Ruth to get ready for the trip to the Hudson Valley. Ivory White and his two other security people and all of their gear have to be loaded up in a nondescript van. Ivory is unhappy that he is not going to be able to be by the side of Devon and Ruth throughout the stay, but even Ivory is hard-pressed to see the likelihood of some sort of attempt by the prophets or other church members to do Devon and Ruth harm. They get a late start and know they will miss the communal breakfast and the first three morning lectures.

"Too bad," Ruth says, laughing, "you know how much I love lectures. Probably going to be some glowing sermons about how happy girls should be to marry a fine old man."

"Try not to dwell on it, Ruth. It is even remotely possible that you will have a good time," Devon says to mollify her.

"I do miss Father and Mother and the kids. I hope they aren't mad at me for not jumping right into nice old Senior Prophet Richland's arms and whooping for joy that I can finally get a husband and not end up as an old maid."

The ballroom holds two hundred twelve people carefully selected to be invited to the retreat. A church choir sings two of the Prophet/President's favorite hymns. Martha looks around and thinks it strange that—of the Council of the Prophets—only her husband Harold has made it. Must be too early for the majority of the senior dignitaries of the church and their families to be there on time. The same seems to hold for the brass from BB&H where Devon works.

"Harold, doesn't it seem a bit strange that only regular members of the church are here? I expect to see a lot of senior people, and look forward to seeing some of the spiritual giants. I sure hope they'll be here. They're so inspiring," Martha says.

The children get restless. It seems to them that it is just like another Sunday full of boring sermons. Besides, they don't see many of their friends, and guess that it is the intent of the retreat to have them get to know the youth from other places in the country, and maybe even the world. It is still boring.

Traffic is a problem, and Devon, Ruth, Ivory, and his two security guards don't reach the Hudson Valley until after ten o'clock. None of them cares much. They presume that the speeches will be boring, and the face-to-face meetings will be traumatic; so, they don't complain as they creep along.

A pastor no one ever heard of from South Africa is the next speaker.

"So we get to listen to the token black, huh?" Angelina, the eldest of the children still living at home, says irreverently.

"You hush, Angelina. That is very rude, and I think it may well be downright racist. Mind your tone, young lady," Martha says in a stage whisper.

Pastor Dumisani Zulu's voice is deep and instantly draws attention. He says, "What a beautiful place...."

Then there is a single click heard only by people near the front. Angelina hears it, then feels a concussion to her entire body. It is the last thing she ever hears. A gardener driving his Japanese import 4x4 Kei Mini-truck full of garden tools and compost hears a deafening explosion, enough to deafen him for the next several hours. The explosion is also enough to throw him and his vehicle fifty feet back along the road. Devon, Katrina, and Ruth Carlisle do not hear anything and are totally shocked when they arrive on the east side of the resort. Devon sees the hapless gardener lying face down on the gravel road. A quick check reveals that he is breathing and has a pulse, but is otherwise more dead than alive. Devon puts in a 911 call; and, within five minutes, three ambulances and ten emergency response vehicles arrive on the scene. It turns out that the gardener is the only witness of the explosion to survive, and he is life-flighted to the Joel A. Halpern level one critical care hospital in Hudson.

Before the police arrive, Devon, Katrina, and Ruth see enough to convince themselves that no one could have survived the horrific explosion that changed the main resort building into a smoking crater a dozen feet deep. Both young women are devastated. Ruth vomits and has to lie down on the grass. Katrina appears dazed and looks fervently to her husband for an explanation. Devon retains enough presence of mind to put in three quick calls—one to McGee, one to Ivory White, and the last one to FBI Special Agent Henry Weintrobe, to inform them what has occurred. McGee, Ivory, and Agent Weintrobe all admonish Devon and Ruth to find a place to be obscure and to wait for them to come for them. Ivory White is the nearest, and he throws gravel into the air as he races from his very recent parking place off the main road to find the only surviving Carlisles parked in a small grove of old-growth elm trees at the edge of the expansive grass plot leading down to the river's edge. Ivory and his heavily armed men surround the young survivors' car and wait for McGee and Weintrobe to arrive. They wait an hour.

In the meantime, the first responders make a quick inspection of the scene and come to the same conclusion as Devon and Ruth—there are no survivors. It is apparent to the fire, rescue, and bomb squad investigators that it will be futile even to look for bodies, let alone survivors. The shift in attitude makes what is left of Quail Run Resort a forensic crime scene. The first priority is to determine the cause of the blast, and the second—following concurrently—is to find DNA. That search will take weeks or months.

Special Agent Weintrobe identifies himself to the first responders and the head of the FBI Emergency Response Team. The ERT leader has assumed command and agrees to have Weintrobe and his agents take the young Carlisle family members to a place of safety.

The agents and McGee's team shepherd the young Carlisles back to the Manhattan safe house where they double-team in an around-the-clock security detail that causes even the blasé New Yorkers in the neighborhood to be curious. Ivory discourages onlookers, the curious, and newsies effectively; and the neighborhood goes back to its usual hectic humdrum. McGee arrives with a doctor and nurse who examine Devon, Katrina, and Ruth and pronounce them psychologically traumatized but otherwise unhurt. The effect of the terroristic scene on Katrina is serious; she can scarcely carry on a conversation and looks to Devon for guidance on even the simplest of decisions and tasks. Ruth's youth serves her well: she is able to cope and be involved in the planning process.

Eight hours pass without word from Annandale. Then Special Agent Garret, head of the FBI ERT unit, calls and talks to Weintrobe.

Special Agent Weintrobe reports to the agents, security guards, and the Carlisles, "At first, the responder teams thought this was more likely than not an accident—a boiler explosion, an ignition of lawn fertilizer, or something like that. But the bomb squad and fire department investigators found evidence of fuse and ignition parts, accelerant residue, and widespread evidence of TNT and Semtex. The bombers must have lined the basement of the main building with explosives. They meant to kill everybody in that resort, and they succeeded except for one worker who is in a coma in the ICU at level one critical care hospital in Hudson. The CSI units—plural—from the FBI and NYPD are going to work around the clock. They have found a few remains, including one hand that looks like it is in good enough condition to allow fingerprinting. DNA processing will take weeks. I'm sorry, but it looks like none of the people attending the retreat survived."

Ruth loses her composure and faints. Katrina weeps, and Devon grits his teeth—more angry than sad for the moment. He blames himself for having agreed to come to the retreat. It is irrational, but then this is an irrational day.

There, but for the grace of God, my entire family would have been killed, he thinks and begins to contemplate what to do next.

A few hours previously the Harold Carlisle nuclear family numbered eighteen persons, and his extended family—including sons, daughters-in-law, and grandchildren—numbered twenty-five. Of all of those people, only three remain alive.

As Devon has his personal moment, Weintrobe steps into the adjoining room and speaks earnestly into his cell phone with Homeland Security. He concludes that call, then gets hold of the data analysis team who have been monitoring the church headquarters of The Only True Church of Christ in Heart of Eden, Wyoming. Then he calls the people assembled in the safe house and brings them up to date on these latest developments.

"We have some pretty conclusive evidence from our listening devices in the Wyoming church," he says. "Our listeners report that voices identified as the president of the church—a guy named Erasmus Jessen—and the man known as Prophet Richland, had a very telling conversation yesterday. We will have to evaluate the recordings to see how clearly they incriminate the cult leaders, but the preliminary evidence is damning. Richland answers a question from the president—Jessen—about plans for the retreat in upstate New York. The conversation goes something like, 'We have a team there today. They are reliable experts. We've used them before without a hitch—no witnesses left, no incriminating evidence, and no ties back to us. I don't think we will have to worry any more about that Carlisle bunch testifying. Dead men tell no tales, I've heard; and there won't be any tales coming from that little get-together.' He goes on to ask Jessen if he wants the rest of the Council of Prophets to be informed, and Jessen tells him yes. He says that it binds everyone together. Our chief analyst tells me that there is a clear—and what appears to be a smoking gun—statement by Jessen. He says, and this is a quote, 'We'll have to name a new prophet to the council very soon.' Richland is heard to give a little laugh."

Devon asks, making an effort to control his temper, "So, what are you and Homeland Security going to do about all of that?"

"Special Agent Todd of HS and I debated that. For now, we are going to put a surveillance team on everybody on that cult council and any other higher-ups you might think appropriate, Devon. We are going to plant a few dozen more listening devices around town, and we have an investigation team going over every piece of evidence to try and learn who the bomb experts were. We have the conspirators; now, we need the triggermen—or women, whatever. We have put every one of the suspects on the FBI's No-Fly list, and every agent in every portal leaving the country has a photograph and description of our suspects."

"A BOLO?" asks Devon.

"Yes," Weintrobe answers. "We expect to send out an APB within the week, and to coordinate a sudden surprise no-knock arrest. Warrants are already in hand. We want to get every one of those murdering cultists, and we want you three to be safe."

"Thanks," Devon says.

He has a few thoughts of his own that he wants to talk to McGee about.

Chapter Nine

M cGee, Devon, Katrina, and Ruth huddle in a conference when the senior law enforcement officers leave
to get ready for the takedown of the murderous cabal.

"I have a thought to run past you, McGee. Katrina, Ruth,
and I have had a chance to consider an idea. We all agree
that arrests and even convictions of the major parties to this
conspiracy will not change the mindset or alter the power
of The Only True Church of Christ. It is based on massive
wealth, and it is international in scope. The only way to stop
them—to neuter them, if you will—is to get at them where
it will hurt the most."

"What do you have in mind, Devon?" McGee asks.

"A major lawsuit. The suit should have two aims: first, to
get an accurate accounting and a public—or at least a courtroom—revelation of the truly incredible wealth and power
of the church. The second aim is to force them to divest a
large percentage of their financial holdings to the plaintiffs—
we remaining Carlisles—enough to take away their power
to corrupt, to exact revenge, and to conduct criminal and

destructive enterprises. We are certainly not junior lawyers, nor are we savvy enough even to know how to go about this. We need you to help us get a law firm that will see the fight to the end, has the know-how and the resources, and is willing to mount a media blitz and anything else that is necessary."

"Are all of you sure? This is your religion, your heritage. There will be no turning back if you file a suit. It could be understood by the lay members that you were subpoenaed and essentially forced to testify in a criminal proceeding, but a civil action is voluntary. Your church practices shunning, does it not?"

Devon decides to let Ruth speak for the three of them.

"All of what you say is true, and all of it is irrelevant. Those people lost all divine authority when they decided to commit murder. It would appear that this was not the first time either. Yes, they practice shunning; it is cruel and demeaning. It divides and destroys families. The church also practices polygamy—young girls marry old men; and many young men have to remain bachelors and be celibate. It is unnatural and cruel. Women are second class citizens, and they are regarded as property. Oh, no, the church never suggests that in public, but in private, it is a different story. Devon is right. Nothing will really change unless the church is so badly hurt financially that it cannot attack; it can only defend. Maybe then the poor deluded members will see that the emperor has no clothes. It's about time."

"You sound angry, and it sounds to me like this is personal—even more personal than the death of your parents and your brothers and sisters," Caitlin says softly.

It is an implicit question.

"You bet it's personal. Do you know what the last thing that I did before going to bed last night, still thinking that all is well? I called Prophet Elias Richland and told him that I would not marry him ever. I was not overcome with so much excitement at the prospect of marrying such an important man—a man who speaks directly to God—no, I told him that the very idea is repugnant and unthinkable. I told him that when I get married, it will be to someone whom I love and who loves me. And, never, never, never, will I even think about being just one of a man's wives, no matter what the religion says."

"Wow," Caitlin says, "Really? How did he react?"

"Actually, not like you'd expect. He was quiet and told me that I certainly had every right to choose for myself. He told me that I would always be in a special place in his heart, and that the friendship of our two families would be as strong as ever. You know, I thought he was laying it on too thick; but he is pretty flowery whenever he speaks."

"Interesting," McGee says.

Immediately prior to receiving the disturbing cell phone call from Ruth Miriam Carlisle, Prophet Richland is in soaring good spirits. He has ensured that the church is safe from prosecution, and that he will be in a better position than ever because the young traitor will never be able to give evidence against him. But the most wonderful thing of all was that he will be able to have the absolutely beautiful and innocent girl as his wife. He has lofty and exciting dreams about that prospect. It was a sure thing; her innocent excitement tells him as much.

That evening, after the fateful call from the wretched ungrateful child, his Elysian dreams crumble into dust. He is just a wrinkled and grey sixty-eight-year-old man after all, and it is destructive to his soul and to his psyche. Elias

Richland has always viewed himself as handsome, and all but irresistible to women. His entire experience with members of the opposite sex has verified that personal image over and over again. Does he not have five altogether willing wives—three of them young enough to be his daughters?

Until that awful call, Elias has always been sure of himself, of the natural world, and that the divinities smiled on him. He is well educated to a point, but his rigidity presents barriers. He understands even the details of Newtonian physics. They explained God's way of controlling the world. Then, a new breed of physicists made everything relative—quantum mechanics, wave versus particulate theory, that dreadful theory of relativity, new subatomic particles being discovered every day, it seems. The universe of physics with its fringed and uncertain edges, unlike the neat fixed numbers of Newton, is a metaphor for his life now. It is a profoundly disturbing realization.

What brings him comfort and the sense once again that all is right with the world is that his last thought as he drifts into an Ambien-induced sleep is that tomorrow, all will be set right again. The Carlisle family will be no more. He smiles at the thought that everybody was wrong when they said, "Hell hath no fury like a woman scorned." The real truth is "Neither heaven nor hell hath any fury to compare to a good man scorned."

Richland gets the news from the people who did his special work fifteen minutes after the deed was done in Annandale. His confidence in himself, and in his God and church are reaffirmed. Like Pollyanna, all is once again right with the world. He has no idea, however, that most of his important confidential communications were being recorded. Nor does he know that the most important member of the Carlisle family has survived intact and now has a crucible-fired and unquenchable purpose....

McGee contacts the senior partner of a famous class action law firm in Los Angeles—Rasmussen, O'Herligy, Rodriguez, and Applewhite. The firm is a very large one, having fourteen satellite offices and more than seven hundred attorneys sweating out their no-social-life existences. David Rasmussen has a reputation for ferocity and a take-no-prisoners philosophy of advocacy for his clients. He has an army of researchers to dig out every negative tidbit to use against his opponents, and is completely lacking in scruples when he seeks out the truth. The truth to him is that set of positive facts that benefits his clients, and lies are everything else. McGee & Associates Investigations served him personally when Rasmussen was sued for legal malpractice by a client corporation who lost a fortune in a hotly contested case. The client's case seemed beyond the reach of legal argument until McGee uncovered that a report used by the plaintiffs in the case had been falsified. Rasmussen was able to find a handwriting expert who confirmed McGee's findings, and David believes that McGee holds an important marker from him.

"David, this is McGee," the private detective says.

"Nice to hear from you, McGee. How are things?"

"Fine. Fine and interesting. I have a very interesting case for you. Besides being interesting, I think you stand to be richer than Croesus once you win the case."

"Ever the con man, right, McGee? 'Have I got a deal for you!'—I hear every time we have a chat."

"And what happens after I tell you that, my friend?"

David laughs heartily, "Justice is done, and I make a bundle. I do have to admit that."

"And this is just another one of those examples."

"So, out with it. What great and noble thing do you bring to me and mine?"

McGee takes the next hour to tell David everything he knows, suspects, and wants. David is hooked from the first couple of sentences.

"I take it that there is real danger to my clients as they pursue the case," David says, and that is all McGee needs to hear.

"Absolutely. I would bet a milk shake that contract killers—or worse, religious zealot killers—will be hot on the trail of the young Carlisle family as soon as the church fathers learn that they are still alive."

"Like when they are served with a suit."

"Yes, like that."

The firm of Rasmussen, O'Herligy, Rodriguez, and Applewhite accepts McGee's proposal that the Carlisles become David's clients. Even before the contract is signed, Devon, Katrina, and Ruth leave New York in the literal dead of night to fly to LAX and their new life in California. There are some misapprehensions that come into play as soon as the Carlisles arrive in Queens and check in at the United counter at IATA—JFK international airport, as it is more popularly known. Every airport, train station, and port in New York and New Jersey is under surveillance by the Brotherhood of Bachelors of The Only True Church of Christ. They are fanatically loyal, and absolutely unquestioning of any directive put out by the prophets—the true vicars of Christ on earth. The Carlisles, the FBI, Homeland Security, and McGee & Associates are all under the misapprehension that the young family's very existence is a secret. They would be chagrined to know that a team of an even dozen members of the Brotherhood are already waiting in the baggage claim area when the Carlisles and Ivory arrive in LAX.

David Rasmussen is operating under a misapprehension of his own. Up until the time of signing of the contract with Devon Carlisle, he believes that he is dealing with a rube—an unfortunate and benighted victim of a cult—whom he must protect and nurture like a fond and powerful uncle. Ivory drives the family to the law firm's offices. That car is preceded by and followed by another security vehicle. No one realizes that they are also being followed by a Baptist Church bus.

After pleasantries, Katrina and Ruth are taken to the safe house—a fortresslike mansion on Mapleton Street in Holmby Hills in Westwood Village. Devon and David get down to cases. David presents the standard contract for the firm that Devon reads. There follows twenty-five minutes of awkward silence as Devon scrutinizes the contract clause by clause and line by line. He hands it back to David.

"It is fine, with one minor exception," Devon says to David, "actually two minor exceptions."

David Rasmussen is an autocrat completely unused to anything but grateful acquiescence from clients who are awed by his phenomenal record in litigation and his domineering personality. He raises his eyebrows

"Yes," Devon continues. "I agree, of course, that no up-front compensation should be received by the law firm. But, the first change I require is in the amount of compensation in the end. The contract calls for a division of 70%-30%, with the thirty percent going to the law firm. The second change relates to the fine-print clause that has the client and the firm sharing expenses equally. I require your firm to absorb 100 percent of the costs."

Devon looks at David as if he has just accomplished a fiat accompli. David disagrees.

"Now, listen, son…," David begins.

"Oh, Mr. Rasmussen, I much prefer to be called Mr. Carlisle, or better, Devon. My father, along with sixteen other members of my family, were killed yesterday in an intentional bombing; that alone should help me gain respect."

David nods his apology, then begins again. "The contract is regular policy throughout the country. We would not be able to work with the arrangement you propose. I realize that you are new to the world of litigation; but I have had very extensive experience; you and your remaining family should just leave the details to me."

"I am young, but believe me I have had a world of experience in the last couple of months. I will never again be able to leave 'the details' to anyone else on a basis of trust. This is business, and I have done my due diligence. Twenty percent to the attorney is common, perhaps equally as common as thirty percent; and I am adamant on that subject. Sharing expenses is almost unheard of in these litigations; all you have to do is turn on your television set to any station— night or day—and you will see the truth of what I am saying. Therefore, sharing expenses is a no-go as well.

"There are powerful incentives for you to take my case, David. It is a slam-dunk; or at least it will become one as soon as a guilty verdict is reached in the criminal portion of the legal proceedings. And…a not inconsequential consideration is that our demand will be for ten billion dollars. I estimate that figure to be a reasonable compensation for my horrendous loss, for your work, and to cripple the vicious intentions of the church," Devon says as matter-of-factly as if he were negotiating a pay package for the purchase of a used car.

David's eyes open wide. He is a quick study and a good judge of character. This young man means what he says. He is obviously adamant about his intentions.

"I have been thinking more on the lines of ten million," David says.

Devon knows he has him since the response to his audacious demands is to shift focus to the eventual award.

"We will open with ten billion. After you do your magic in negotiation, we might come down to eight billion. That, however, will depend on what the forensic accounting turns up."

"You no longer seem like a young man to me, Devon. Your demands will cost me a bundle; so, I am going to have to talk to my partners. Give me half an hour, all right?"

"Sure."

David has no intention of talking to his partners. This is his case, and he will make the decisions. However, he does need to get a better feel of what this case is about, including enlightenment about his interesting client. He calls McGee.

"Hello, David," McGee answers on his private line.

"Good afternoon, McGee. I have a question about your take on Devon Carlisle."

He describes the ongoing conversation with his potential client.

"Is he for real? I mean, if I give in to his demands, will he see it all the way to the end? It is going to get a lot rougher, I fear. Are you sure the cult has that much money—ten billion is far from chump change, and no judge will ever allow a judgment that takes practically all of the defendant's assets. Do they have thirty or forty billion dollars?"

"As to yours and my client, yes, he is genuine—well-educated, financially savvy, very bright, stubborn, unemotional, and tough, at least so far. I have seen a lot of the financial evidence. Not only does the cult have that much money, but they are majority shareholders in several companies. This can easily turn into a class action case. If it does, there is precedent for taking all of their money and assets—remember the Southern Poverty Law Center cases against white supremacist groups like The Order in Washington, The White Aryan Resistance in Oregon, and the Kluckers. This cult can be a money tree for your firm. You would be penny wise and pound foolish to pass on it over the minor costs of doing business with the Carlisle family."

David does not need any more of a tutorial. He thanks McGee, invites his firm to be in charge of the civil forensic investigation into the cult's finances, and to supervise security for the Carlisles and the law firm's team. Then he goes back into the conference room and accedes to all of Devon Carlisle's demands. Lawyer and client agree that it is strategically better to wait until the end of the last day of the expected criminal trial to file the suit. Both David and Devon are home in time for supper.

Chapter Ten

Three days after the Annandale bombing, the Council of Prophets meets in the chapel headquarters of the religion in Heart of Eden, Wyoming. The crime scene tapes are now gone, and there is a unanimous "good-riddance" feeling among the church leaders; and a hope that this is the last they will see of the U.S. federal government in action.

Prophet/President Jessen now feels safe to express himself frankly and to permit the other six members to do the same during this seminal meeting. His sense of ease comes from the fact that the company hired by the church to identify and to remove listening devises was very thorough, and equally successful. Eight devices were taken away. No one on the council is aware that there are seven other bugging devices in the conference room alone, and more than thirty spread around the town.

"We will have an accounting from the New York firm we have used for our 'special services' needs for several years. The Quail Run project was handled by them. I will take the conference call in exactly one minute. Please hold questions until the end of the company's presentation," Jessen says.

The conference call arrangements work perfectly.

"Hello, President," a harsh male voice says with a thick New Jersey accent.

"Hello, Leader. Let us not waste each other's time. You were ninety-nine percent successful, but three very significant targets escaped."

"Not from our device, they didn't. If those people are alive, that means that they were not yet in the building."

"We happen to know that you are correct in that assumption, Leader. We have located them in a very well-secured mansion in a place called Holmby Hills in Los Angeles. Our surveillance team has evaluated the situation thoroughly, and it will be extremely difficult—if not impossible—to arrange a ... meeting. We want you to link up with our people in Los Angeles and provide them with your advice and expertise."

"Wet?"

"Yes. Probably a sniper."

"When?"

"ASAP, but plans cannot include us or reverberate back to us. It would look best if the untimely deaths of the three Carlisles were to appear to be accidental, but that may be just wishful thinking. The intensity of the security measures rivals anything the FBI has ever done—it is on a par with the secret service protection of the president. You have some leeway because our real deadline is that they need to disappear before they get on the stand to testify against us."

"Same payment arrangements as for our previous missions?"

"Yes."

"Done," and the phone call terminates.

"Now, we will meet the Los Angeles watchers in person and find out the details of their surveillance of the Carlisles over the past three days. Please call them in, Mrs. Casper."

Three casually dressed men and one woman enter the council's conference room.

"Has the place been debugged?" is the first thing out of the mouth of the woman who has obviously been elected to be the spokesperson.

"Certainly. We have top-notch security; and, in fact they found several listening devices. So share the latest on the three Carlisles. They need to be dealt with before we are detained by law enforcement; at least, I think my pessimism is well founded," Jessen says.

"They were taken to a safe house. Apparently, there is a lot of money going into their safe-keeping. Are you by any chance familiar with Holmby Hills in Los Angeles, brothers?"

"A place of great riches and decadence," says Elias Richland.

"And a place of serious power and influence. We think it unlikely that we can get at them in the house, and we will probably have to put a tail on them and find some sort of pattern to set up an ambush. That is likely to take some time."

"I have been inspired by the Lord that there is very little time. We must act promptly. I am sure of that," Richland says.

"Well, Prophet Richland, there is one thing we could try. We have located a tree that overlooks the property wall where we have placed a watcher. We can substitute a sniper. It might be worth a try."

The Prophet/President speaks up, "A miss would alert the police that we are aware that the Carlisles are alive and that we know their location. I presume that security would become even more intense."

"There are always risks, your Holiness, but we have former Delta Ranger snipers who are tough and patient enough to sit silently in amongst the tree branches for a few days. They are being paid well, and perhaps it is time for them to earn their keep," says the woman from Los Angeles.

"Will you need an advance?" Richland asks.

"I'm afraid so. The snipers and their escape people will have to be paid in advance, because they will have to disappear immediately after they fire the first shot."

"Can we trust them?" the prophet/president asks.

"Absolutely."

"Then, here's the money. Use it wisely. It is sacred tithing money from the faithful. The Lord will expect that His will and His funds are obeyed and respected."

A single cell phone call to a number with a Westwood Village prefix sets the plan into motion.

In the Winder Dairy van parked half a block away, the unified Homeland Security and FBI SWAT unit is recording every word coming from the church conference room, and the six senior officers are listening in real time.

"Heard enough?" Special Agent Henry Weintrobe asks his HS counterpart, Clarke Todd.

"It'll hold up. I'd rather we take them down for conspiracy to commit murder instead of another actual murder. We have enough on them from the tapes to get convictions for the bombing mass murders. Let's go after them."

Weintrobe goes to the all-agents signal and speaks three words: "It's a go."

The unified team has worked feverishly for the five days following the raid on BB&H, and has a clear, objective, and detailed plan in place. A hundred agents in thirty vehicles, including heavy armored trucks and supreme specialty bomb squad vehicles driven to Heart of Eden from the manufacturing plant in Clerburne, Texas, have been waiting for orders. It is an extremely dark night with the moon and stars obscured by heavy storm clouds. The "go" order puts an army—"the cavalry," as they call themselves—into well-coordinated motion.

Every ingress and egress is blocked. The church campus is surrounded. The URT [Urgent Response Teams]—four of them—advance on foot moving stealthily but in double time. They are armed with night-vision goggles, multiple copies of warrants and subpoenas—including subpoenas duces tecum for any and all records—and they are armed sufficiently to carry out an assault on any of a number of small nations.

Weintrobe says—more to himself than to anyone else—"*This will not be another Wacky Waco fiasco. Not on my watch!*"

The members of the Council of the Prophets and the watchers from Los Angeles are stupefied by a sudden coordinated attack. SWAT officers toss flashbangs into the conference room and crash in through every window and door in the room, screaming "Federal Agents!" "Police!" and "Wyoming State police!" and rush the thoroughly cowed people in the room. Weintrobe and Todd follow close behind.

The only casualty is a bruised shin on one HS special agent who cannot see well enough in the choking smoke. Within minutes, all of the members of the Council of the Prophets, their servants, and the three plotters from Los Angeles are in custody and walking the perp walk into waiting paddy wagons for the benefit of seventy-five newspaper, radio, television, and internet reporters brought in for the occasion. Weintrobe is captured in a perfect pose handing the subpoenas to the familiar media personality, Prophet/President Erasmus Jessen.

The former Delta Force sniper has been bored to distraction sitting in a backbreaking position in a tree on a very affluent location for the past two days—Mapleton Street, in Holmby Hills, Westwood Village, in Los Angeles. His cell phone vibrates. There is no caller ID and no voice message. The text message reads simply, "NOW." It is a propitious moment. The sniper has a good photo of Devon Carlisle, and the man is making the stupidest mistake a target can make. He stands inside looking out of a third story window of what is obviously a bedroom. The room is brightly lit behind him. The sniper ignores his stiffness, hunger, thirst, and the discomfort of his perch. He takes a deep breath and places the crosshairs of his rifle on the T zone of Carlisle's face—the perfect kill site because it guarantees that the high-energy rifle bullet will pass through the man's upper nose between the eyes and cause a biological explosion in his medulla oblongata. He switches the laser site on and sees the precise red point sit dead center on Carlisle's nasion.

He slowly and calmly exhales; and, as he does, he begins the slow, practiced squeeze of the trigger on his finely tuned weapon equipped with a well sighted-in night optics rifle scope. In the room, Ivory White sees the red dot on his client's forehead and hurtles himself into Devon. Devon goes to the floor with Ivory on top of him. The soft-core bullet passes exactly where the sniper aims but where Devon's face is now missing and harmlessly takes out an expensive Tang Dynasty vase. Within ten seconds, watchdogs and a dozen agents are racing towards the sniper's tree.

Knowing that he will only get off the one shot, the sniper drops out of the tree and sprints for the corner of Mapleton Street where a supercharged BMW is waiting. The black racing car roars into the night with the sniper and his driver essentially invisible behind illegally deep black tinted windows. The security agents are too late, and the get-away car vanishes into the gloom.

Devon is shaken up but otherwise unhurt. Ivory banged his head on the sharp edge of a bedside table and has a cut that will require sutures, but he has had worse and he is all right. The two Carlisle women are panicked, but a tough and experienced woman member of Ivory's "Special Services" staff calms them down.

Chapter Eleven

June 2017

Like the O.J. Simpson trial in 1994–1995—characterized as the most publicized trial in American history—the so-called "Trial of the Prophets" in the United States District Court for the District of Wyoming in Casper captures enormous pretrial media attention, a paparazzi-feeding frenzy, and viewer involvement that borders on addiction and salacious guilty pleasure.

Simpson was arrested June 17, 1994 for the murder of his wife and her male friend, thus starting the worldwide fascination with the legal proceedings. The jury was sworn in on November 2; opening statements were presented on January 24, 1995; and the verdict was announced October 3, 1995. From arrest to verdict, the Simpson murder case was in the news without let up for over eighteen months.

The six "Prophets" and over a hundred other members of The Only True Church of Christ are arrested on August 18, 2015, and the wheels of justice move through a dizzying series of legal motions and countermotions, interrogations and grants of immunity, quick trials for a variety of crimes less than murder, and the development of an audience following and market share comparable to the Simpson circus. There are seven postponements—most coming at the demand of stellar group of famous defense attorneys—before the district court Judge Samuel T. Groman finally halts the manipulations and sets the trial date in stone for June 2, 2017. By that time, the defendant list for the murder trial has been winnowed down to nine individuals to sit at the bar of justice in the previously sleepy Wyoming town.

All hotel and motel rooms, private residences willing to take in renters at confiscatory rates, and trailer spaces, are filled to overflowing by the middle of May. A tent city springs up in the outskirts of Casper reminiscent of the boom-and-bust era of oil wildcatting in the area decades earlier. Local residents have difficulty trying to buy groceries, get to work, or drive their cars. Their patience at being accosted by media people comes to an end by the last week in May. The town has taken on a circus appearance altogether similar to that in Dayton, Tennessee, during the 1925 Scopes Monkey Trial.

Crowd control is well beyond the capacity of local Casper police. On the opening day of the trial, contingents of police from neighboring towns, state troopers, FBI agents, and finally, Wyoming National Guard, are required to hold back the hordes of onlookers, conspiracy theorists, religious zealots, and anti-cult demonstrators. Feelings are at a fever pitch, and the mayor of Casper and the governor of Wyoming fear that a riot will break out as soon as the first news is broadcast from the courtroom.

The reality in the courtroom is 180 degrees opposite to the frenzy outside. Immediately after the judge gavels the court to order, the prosecution makes a stunning motion. The defense team stands in full agreement.

Wilber Forestall, the federal prosecutor, announces, "Your honor, the prosecution and the defense have arrived at a plea agreement for the defendants. The marshal has a copy for you. In short, the plea agreement stipulates full allocution of all wrongdoing in return for the government removing the death penalty and the reduction of charges for six of the nine defendants, dropping of all charges against the family members of all defendants, and removal of prosecution for violations of RICO statutes. The six defendants agree to prison terms of fifteen to twenty-five years and to fines of one million dollars each. The three remaining defendants agree to accept full responsibility for their crimes—including conspiracy to commit first-degree murder, money laundering, operating a career criminal enterprise, theft by fraud, violations of federal statutes for bigamy, and felony child abuse including several counts rape of several minor boys and girls."

It takes Judge Groman several minutes to absorb the enormity of this reversal in the progress of the trial.

"Does the defense agree?"

"We do, you honor."

Groman then closely questions all nine defendants.

Each of them hangs his head and answers, "Yes."

"Please speak up for the court recorder."

"Yes!" they say in fully audible unison.

"The plea is accepted. Marshals, remove the prisoners. Court is adjourned."

McGee is as dumbfounded as anyone. He calls Los Angeles where the Carlisles and his partners are waiting for news.

He tells them about the abrupt end to the trial, and sums up the effect and the mood in the Wyoming farm town,

"It reminds me of the T.S. Eliot poem written in 1925 as a commentary on the signing of the Treaty of Versailles—*The Hollow Men*—'This is the way the world ends. This is the way the world ends. Not with a bang but a whimper.'"

The response from the crowd of enthusiasts standing in the streets of Casper and by the media is more a bang than a whimper; but everyone realizes that the show is over; and the events surrounding the criminal proceedings are largely forgotten after the next five-day news cycle begins. The criminal proceedings are, however, only the beginning salvo in the fight.

In the Los Angeles law offices of Rasmussen, O'Herligy, Rodriguez, and Applewhite, congratulations and celebratory flutes of expensive champagne are shared; then the attorneys and the plaintiffs get down to work. They make one last review of the complaint and the brief that is already drafted. The complaint is a technical exercise, and the lawyers use the simplified process available in Los Angeles for creating judicial council forms. They are available online. Agreement is a foregone conclusion, and David Rasmussen asks his office assistant to enter the fifteen billion-dollar Carlisle v. The Only True Church of Christ, et al. civil suit into the system.

Because of the magnitude of the damages requested and the media's extreme interest, the case is put on a fast track. The plaintiffs are prepared and gracefully accept the acceleration. The defendants consider that they have been ambushed and respond with a series of delaying motions. Those motions are considered by the judge—William Oxford-Randelle—of the Superior Court of California, County of Los Angeles, to be without foundation. The civil trial is scheduled in the Stanley Mosk Courthouse on Hill Street in downtown L.A. for November 23, 2017.

Chapter Twelve

August 12, 2017

O ne of the attempts by the defense in Carlisle v. The Only True Church of Christ, et al. is to keep plaintiff Devon Carlisle from attending the first in the series of depositions of the defendants. It is argued that Devon is on the witness list for the trial and therefore could learn defense strategy and change his testimony accordingly. David Rasmussen argues that Devon has been present throughout the case from pre-arrest investigation and supplying law enforcement, the defense, the plaintiffs' attorneys, and the court with documentary evidence. He has reviewed a complete and unabridged video of the criminal trial—such as it was—in the federal district court in Wyoming. Five days before the deposition, Judge Oxford-Randelle rules in favor of Devon's attendance under evidence code 777§.

The day is insufferably hot, and the atmosphere in the law offices of Rasmussen, O'Herligy, Rodriguez, and Applewhite is near the boiling point. Prophet/President and now federal prisoner #48120-0929 in the United States Penitentiary, Terre Haute, Indiana, Erasmus Jessen, has been delivered by prison bus from Indiana to California. He has been shackled the entire way, and the bus is one of an older vintage that lacks air-conditioning. He is out of sorts—way out—by the time his unfeeling federal guards push him into a chair. His shackles are left in place over the objections of his attorneys.

The swearing in does not go well. Jessen refuses to acknowledge the jurisdiction of California or even the United States over him, since he is God's man and need not answer to anyone else. Rasmussen and Jessen's lead attorney, Joseph Taylor Barlow, have an off-the-record conversation that is sobering to Barlow whose résumé includes the defense of FLDS Prophet Warren Jeffs (a failure). With full deference and courtesy, Rasmussen lets Barlow know that if Prisoner Jessen is taken out of the deposition room, the plaintiff's attorneys will contact Judge Oxford-Randelle for an immediate summary judgment. They plan to demand the full fifteen billion dollars requested in the suit.

Barlow sneers at Rasmussen's challenge and counters that he will call the judge right now.

Rasmussen only hears Barlow's end of the conversation:

"Your Honor, I am loathe to bother you with such a trivial matter, but I have no choice. As you know, I represent Prophet/President Erasmus Jessen…."

Pause.

"Yes, Your Honor, I do understand that. If you insist, I will call him Mr. Jessen. However, your identifying him as Federal Prisoner #48120-0929 might appear prejudicial."

Pause.

"All right, your honor, he is Mr. Jessen from here on out. Thank you. To the point, Mr. Jessen is refusing to testify in the deposition. He denies that earthly governments and courts have no power to question, to try, or to punish him…."

Pause

"Yes, sir. Of course I understand that his opinion is irrelevant as to the rule of law here in the real world of the United States and California."

Pause.

"I will try, Your Honor. However, my worthy opponent states that he will seek a summary judgment this very day for the full amount of the suit—an outlandish sum of fifteen billion dollars—if Mr. Jessen continues to defy the court."

Pause.

"But, your honor, that deprives my client of his rights to a fair trial. Neither he nor the church has anything like that sort of money. It would bankrupt The Only True Church of Christ without due process."

Pause.

"Admittedly, it remains to be determined by evidence from both sides to the finder-of-fact, the jury, whether or not my statement or that of the plaintiffs in the case are true."

"I see, but of course we would have to appeal."

Pause.

"I understand, Your Honor. Placing that sum in escrow while the cogs and wheels of the appeals process would technically be legal, but…."

Pause.

"I will have to concede. We have to accept the lesser of evils. I will work to persuade my clients—my three clients."

Pause.

"I will do my best to get it done today; and yes, I have to admit that today is as good as any other time. Thank you, sir."

Barlow glares daggers at Rasmussen and gets out of his chair without a comment to the opposing attorney. Still in off-the-record status, David, Devon, and the court recorder leave the room to Barlow, Jessen, and the two prison guards. Shouting can be heard, but it is not possible to make out actual conversation.

David maintains his annoyingly placid composure, and Devon takes a cue from him.

Twenty minutes later, the deposition resumes. Jessen is sworn in, although he acts as if his hand on the Bible is going to be burned.

The deposition is long, and David is polite and correct, but exhaustively thorough.

At three o'clock, after an hour's break for lunch, David begins to make the first of his several most inflammatory demands.

"Mr. Jessen, within one week from now, we will have from you a complete accounting of the holdings of your cult…."

"Come now, Mr. Rasmussen, let's keep it civil. The Only True Church of Christ is a legally recognized religious organization. Let's keep it simple and courteous and only refer to the institution as 'The Church' and leave out the pejoratives," objects Barlow.

Rasmussen nods and asks Jessen, "Would you like me to repeat the question, sir?"

"Not necessary," Jessen replies. "The answer is no."

"No, what?" Rasmussen asks as if he does not know.

"We will never divulge our church's sacred records. Never. You have no right."

"Mr. Jessen, Mr. Barlow, this requests goes to the heart of our suit. Since we are on a fast track to the trial in chief, we will request a hearing on this request before the day is out."

"We would like to have a recess, Mr. Rasmussen. My client is tired and needs some refreshment. It is three fifteen and getting late in the day. Perhaps we should adjourn for now and resume tomorrow."

"Three fifteen in the afternoon is not 'late,' Mr. Barlow. And Mr. Jessen appears to be just fine to me. Let's say half an hour of rest and refreshment then we return to the question at hand. Or, would you rather have another discussion with Judge Oxford-Randelle?

David's question is posed with a saccharine sweet expression.

Barlow knows that another call to the judge would just annoy the man, and he must avoid such a foolhardy action. However, he knows that he cannot allow the plaintiffs to get hold of those records. Plaintiffs all over the world have been seeking such information from corporations including churches, and almost every time, the organization chooses to cave in and settle. The Roman Catholic Church has settled child abuse and church failure to protect cases in North and South America and in multiple countries in Europe to the tune of multiple billions of dollars in order to protect information about the church's vast financial empire that would leave it wide open to the next plaintiff and the next and the next, until the Catholic church would have to close its doors.

The same question came up in the series of suits against the FLDS; the polygamous church never divulged its finances, but the expense was huge. It was a fairly recent frame of reference for the attorney for the defense.

"My client and I will have to have a conference, and I will have to call the other defendants again. Give us an hour."

"All right, but we will hold you to an hour. This question and several more will be settled today, one way or the other," Rasmussen says, and his face and body language convey the certainty that the gloves are off and the much aggrieved plaintiffs are in no mood to compromise.

When Barlow, Jessen, and the two burly prison guards return, they look anything but refreshed. Their faces tell what has gone on, and Devon and David can hardly wait to learn what they will hear.

"Mr. Rasmussen…."

"Let me remind you, Mr. Barlow, we are back on the record."

"Fine. Now allow me to finish. To spare everyone further difficulty, my clients have graciously agreed to proceed to a settlement of the case."

Although it is not entirely unexpected, it still comes as something of a shock.

"You have our full attention, Mr. Barlow."

"Of course, we admit no guilt."

"The question of guilt is moot, sir. Your clients—all of them—have admitted in criminal court to their crimes, both physical and financial; and they are currently serving prison terms."

Barlow ignores Rasmussen's comment.

"As I was saying, Mr. Rasmussen, we admit no guilt. We will not divulge the church's financial status, and everything agreed upon in this settlement will be sealed and never allowed to come to the attention of the public. Finally, we must have an agreement that no personal finances or family finances will be involved."

We'll see about that, both David Rasmussen and Devon Carlisle think to themselves, but they do not interrupt the flow.

"And is there some sort of concession that you intend to make from your side, or is it only the plaintiffs who will once again be brutalized?" David asks, his face and voice no longer placid or collegial.

"Of course," Barlow says quickly, "I am getting to that. The church is not as rich as you might have been thinking, but we have come to the decision to make a most generous offer. We can write a check for fifty million dollars here and now, and the case is over."

David and Devon look at each other, and, as if following a script, break into hard, sardonic laughter, their faces fixed in scornful disbelief and distrust.

The facial expressions are not lost on Barlow. He expects a counter.

"The settlement price is fifteen billion dollars, Mr. Barlow. Your offer is an insult, and is woefully inadequate," David says, his voice hard with bitter anger.

Jessen speaks up and addresses his comments to Devon.

"You, of all people, know the finances of the church. You know the good we do. You know that the brethren and I want you to come back into the fold. Let us both repent, and you choose Christian kindness in dealing with this unholy legal mess. You know our love for you and your wife and sister. Let us settle like brothers and make up. At least, you can approach this from a fair business point of view."

"No. Let me give an accounting. The church has assets in excess of forty billion dollars. I know that from my own accounting work. I have no doubt that you have squirreled away billions more. That is not even the half of it: you murdered my entire family except for three persons. You have blackened our names. You have attempted to kill me at least once. Your side of the balance of justice is grossly heavier than mine, my wife's, and my sister's. Money will not bring my beautiful and loving family back, but enough will ensure your weakness and inability to hurt people any more. It will never balance the scales entirely, but at least it will be a token for the lives of those good people. The final amount is fifteen billion dollars. So far as I am concerned, fifteen billion dollars lets you and your vile cult off easy; and if you can't negotiate in good faith, we are done. We'll see you in court and make everything a matter of public record."

"Now, now, let's take it easy," Barlow soothes. "Perhaps we could increase the offer somewhat. Now, gentlemen, what do you really think is fair?"

David answers, "Full disclosure of all finances of the church, and the plaintiffs receive seventy-five percent of the assets. That applies even if church property has to be liquidated to serve the debt."

Barlow and Jessen hold a hurried whispered private conference.

"All right, a billion dollars. That is confiscatory and evil, but we will have to bear the cross."

Devon stands up. "We're done here. The final offer is full disclosure and eighty percent of the church assets. Speak again and our generosity will cease, and we will go for ninety percent in front of a jury of twelve people honest and true. Lots of luck for you to make your case to them."

He collects his papers and starts for the door.

David starts to speak to him, "Devon, perhaps we could look at some area of compromise."

The attorney in him makes David fear that walking out now would result in the potential goose failing to lay an egg of any value.

To his surprise and chagrin, Devon shoots him a threatening look, and David has a small shiver of fear, something like he felt the first day he and Devon met. He waits to see what Devon has in mind.

Devon walks out the conference room door. David quickly gets up and follows him out.

When the door closes, Devon abruptly turns on his attorney.

"David, do not lose your courage. This is not over. And do not ever make an offer without running it by me first. Finally–and for as long as we have a business association–never suggest that we are in disagreement or that we are going to accept a paltry settlement. You need to get rich from this. I need to disable that unholy church—that cult—forever. Do you understand me?"

"Sure, Devon, but I am not at all sure you can push them any further."

"It's we, David. If it is not we, then we will part company."

"Do you want to make a counteroffer, Devon? We are in a Mexican stand-off right now. It's getting late, and I am afraid that they will bolt and take their chances. That will result in protracted and interminable delays. We are likely not to see any real money for years, maybe decades."

"I disagree. I think Judge Oxford-Randelle has about had it with the criminals. We do not have to make a case beyond a reasonable doubt, just to the level of the preponderance of evidence being in our favor."

"That's true, Devon, but I do think it is our time to make a counteroffer. Hear me out," says David.

After their talk, the two men return to the conference room and make an offer that they genuinely hope will be accepted even if everybody has to choke on it a little.

Chapter Thirteen

The same day, 4:00 PM, Pacific Standard Time.

It is only the third time that Katrina and Ruth have left the house. They need to relieve the mounting tension knowing that the negotiations are underway in their attorneys' offices. Their minders from McGee's office and from the FBI are fully vigilant and unapproving of the outing.

Ivory White and the special agent on duty with him reconnoiter the restaurant. Ed Rainer and the other FBI agent stay in the car with the women.

"I suppose it looks okay," says Ivory, "but it doesn't feel okay."

"Yeah, let's get it over with," says the FBI agent who is ready to put his life on the line for these potential material witnesses, but he is not enthusiastic to do so.

He signals the two security men in the car, and they bring the women into the air-conditioned coolness of the restaurant that the FBI and HS agents have vetted. The waiter asks what they would like to drink.

Ivory says, "We're ready to order. We're in something of a hurry."

Katrina and Ruth don't like it, but they know they have to follow the orders from their personal security guards; so, they don't protest.

Everyone gives simple, quick requests; so, they won't be any longer than absolutely necessary. The joy of being out of the house is ruined anyway.

Ten minutes later, the waiter returns with hamburgers and French fries, and two plates of fish and chips. There is one odd thing about the large round platter that the waiter holds with his left hand. Everything, even the metal dome plate covers, is lying under a large starched white cloth. Ivory's senses quicken.

He is faster than the two FBI agents. The waiter sets the platter down on a trolley table then whips of the tablecloth covering the platter, lifts off one of the metal covers, and extracts a 9 mm hand gun. The two agents reach for their weapons, but the waiter shoots one of them in the heart and whips his weapon in the direction of the other agent and Ivory.

The women are frozen in shock.

Ivory reacts automatically, and his gun is out and firing before the waiter can get off a second shot. Ivory puts three rounds into the waiter in the Mozambique pattern—two midchest, and one in the center of the killer's forehead. As he falls, the infuriated agent who is uninjured pumps all nine rounds of his .357 Magnum into the man's body, six of them when he is lying on the floor. In the post-shooting interrogation by the OPR [Office of Professional Responsibility], the agent is asked why he pumped a full nine rounds into the suspect.

His reply is classical: "Because I ran out of bullets."

The Rapid Response Team arrives on scene and secures it, alert to the chance of finding any co-conspirators. Two armored vehicles whisk the Carlisle women out of danger and back to the safe house. The investigation reveals that a GPS tracker has been attached to the undercarriage of the FBI vehicle. It falls to Ivory to inform McGee of the attack, and to McGee to tell Devon and David what has happened. The report is conveyed shortly before they return to the conference room. Devon is furious.

He walks directly over to Jessen and says, "Stand up. I have a message."

Jessen believes he is looking Death in the face, and he knows why. He stands up.

The two lawyers move to restrain Devon, but he will have none of it.

"You had a killer come after my wife and sister. He killed an FBI agent, and the other guards killed him. Now we will come to a final settlement. Here is what is going to happen before you have your chat with the FBI, which incidentally, does not take at all kindly to the killing of one of its agents.

"You will sign a paper guaranteeing to turn over twelve billion dollars right now. I have the account number here. You will give a full written accounting to Judge Oxford Randelle of your cult's finances. If twelve billion is less than two-thirds of the total church holdings and your personal fortune, the judge is directed by you to release the amount that comes to the whole two-thirds. The judge will hold the right to increase that award to ninety percent of your ill-gotten and evil money if another attack or even an accident—like I fall down the stairs—should occur. In exchange, I will plead that you get to live out your life in solitary confinement but avoid the death penalty."

Erasmus Jessen cringes and looks down at his lap. He is afraid. He wants to live, and he knows—or at least, he believes—that the demonic young man standing over him holds his life in his hands.

"I'll sign. Just keep him away from me," he whimpers.

No one consults with the codefendants, and no one protests to the judge that there is coercion. It would have done no good, because the FBI has found incontrovertible evidence that Jessen and his crony, Elias Richland, hired the hit man who killed the FBI agent from their prison cells. The judge is perfectly happy to finalize the bargain that everyone knows will cripple The Only True Church of Christ, hopefully bringing an end to the violence. He is more than willing to up the ante as Devon demands if another attack occurs from anyone.

Chapter Fourteen

July 2019

There are many interesting aspects to coming into great wealth suddenly. Ask any winner of a major lottery. The largest lottery annuity jackpot was $656 million from the Mega Millions lottery in March 2012—the winner took the single payout which was still the largest cash payout in U.S. history, $474 million. Spain's *Sorteo Extraordinario de Navidad* [Spanish Christmas Lottery] is the world's largest lottery. In 2012, the main jackpot was €720 million—$941.8 million USD, which came from a total prize pool of €2.52 billion—$3.297 billion USD. Unlike the situation in the United States—where lottery winnings are taxed—European jackpots are generally tax-free, although the lotteries themselves are taxed. European jackpots are paid in a lump sum.

There is no escaping the notoriety of the incredible monetary windfall that the three surviving members are awarded. The final agreement approved by Judge William Oxford-Randelle includes an iron-clad clause of secrecy concerning the final amount—$12 billion—to be transferred to the Carlisles in four payments over one year. The judge intends that the amount will handicap but not destroy the church. Only he knows the actual wealth of the religious organization, and he holds that information to be inviolate so long as no further attacks are mounted against the plaintiffs. The activities of transferring money from the church to the Carlisles and from the Carlisles to various financial institutions, charities, and foundations lead several intrepid investigative reporters to make fairly educated guesses of the actual amounts involved.

The reporters overestimate the final prize because they fail to factor in the friendly visits from the IRS. Ordinarily, financial awards for settlements that do not involve physical injury are not taxable, which is the case in Carlisle v. The Only True Church of Christ, et al. However, both the judge and the IRS conclude that the settlement payments are for punitive damages. Such damages are taxable. They are awarded—by definition—to the plaintiff in order to punish a defendant and to forestall the defendant or others from committing similar acts. The damages awarded are contingent upon the Carlisles proving the desirability or the necessity of awarding them. In the Carlisle case, the offense was proved beyond any reasonable doubt to have been committed knowingly, deliberately, and related to negligent and fraudulent behavior on the part of the church. The amount received for punitive damages is payable even though no physical injury occurred in any of the three survivors. The wrongful deaths of the rest of the family were dealt with by the criminal court system.

The three Carlisles did not cry all the way to the bank; of the money that finally comes into their possession—after taxes, payments to the law firm of Rasmussen, O'Herligy,

Rodriguez, and Applewhite, and settling up with McGee—they share equal thirds of $3,740,000,000. The law firm celebrates their twenty-percent share—which comes to $960 million—and McGee & Associates shared their one million dollar fee. The litigation division at Rasmussen's firm spends a year developing its class action suit that promises them another billion. McGee & Associates are still the investigators and stand to earn another million a year for three years.

The inevitable newly discovered family members, friends, investment hucksters, con artists, and unfortunates—who come out of the woodwork and the hinterlands—lay their claims and harass Devon, Katrina, and Ruth. The biggest threat to their financial gains and to their well-being would likely come from the development of intemperate lifestyles; so, they seek further counsel from the Rasmussen, O'Herligy, Rodriguez, and Applewhite firm—this time from Crandall Applewhite, the head of the corporate law division.

The first thing Applewhite does is to give some very pertinent advice:

"Lottery winners and people who win significant awards in court first need some space. This is going to be a new life, and you need to prepare for it. Change your address, telephone number, e-mail addresses, and passwords, and only share them with people who need to know and who earn your trust. Let me help you gain some anonymity from financial predators and let McGee and David help protect against the cult predators. Our division has an excellent estate attorney, and now is the time to use her.

"The next thing we need to do is to develop a living, investment, and charity strategy for both the short and the long-term. I suggest that each of you keep separate estates since your tastes and needs differ. Your investments may parallel or cross each other, but they do not need to be exactly the same. I am going to advise all of you to take a full one-third of your total estate right now and put it into very safe, relatively low-yield, investments like municipal bonds, especially those that are tax exempt. Use that money to buy the things you need, then the things you want, and to have fun. The next one-third can be directed towards more adventuresome investments—the ones you can afford to lose. The last one-third should be put into a good safe charitable foundation, and maintain close scrutiny on it and its managers. You have plenty of time to decide—or to help decide—who or what should receive your generosity.

"Finally, some general advice: don't go crazy; get some rest; watch your backs. The cult has not gone away."

Applewhite requires the three Carlisles to learn from the many lottery winners whose lives were ruined by their sudden riches.

"A naturalized citizen from India who lived in Chicago won $1 million with a lump sum payout of $450K. He died the next day of cyanide poisoning, presumably a homicide. Jack Whittaker was the wealthiest man ever to win a major lottery jackpot. He was already worth some $17 million when he won a $315 million Powerball jackpot in December 2002. Whittaker, pledging to give ten percent of his fortune to Christian charities, donated $14 million to his own Jack Whittaker Foundation, and gave a new house, a new Dodge Ram Truck, and $50,000 in cash to the woman who worked at the convenience store where he purchased his winning ticket. Soon after he won the huge jackpot, he developed serious legal difficulties and personal problems; he became an alcoholic and began to go to strip clubs. In 2003, thieves stole $545,000 from his car while he was in a West Virginia strip club parking lot. In 2007, Whittaker learned that thieves had completely emptied his bank accounts. In 2004, his car was robbed again, that time for $200,000. He had a series of personal tragedies including overdose deaths of his beloved granddaughter and her boyfriend. Finally, Whittaker himself alleged that he was broke. He failed to pay a woman who successfully sued him and was also sued by Caesars Atlantic City casino for paying his $1.5 million of gambling debts with rubber checks.

"Billie Bob Harrell, Jr. won the $31 million Texas Lotto jackpot in 1997. He quit his job, vacationed in Hawaii, donated tens of thousands of dollars to his church, bought cars and houses for friends and family, and donated 480 turkeys to the poor. But, here is the lesson—Harrell's lavish spending attracted the wrong kind of attention. He had to change his phone number several times after strangers called to *demand* donations. He made a bad deal with a company that gives lottery winners lump-sum payments in exchange for their annual checks. He ended up with less money than he had won. Harrell and his wife separated less than a year later. His son found him dead inside his home from a self-inflicted gunshot wound in May 1999.

"William Post III won $16.2 million in the Pennsylvania lottery in 1988. The man succumbed to his own and to strangers' vices: he fell victim to crime, bankruptcy, tragedy, and incredibly poor spending habits. Within two weeks of receiving his first annual payment of nearly $500,000, he purchased a restaurant, a used-car lot, and an airplane which squandered two-thirds of his first check. Within three months—as difficult as it is to comprehend—he was $500,000 in debt. He literally could not buy a piece of good luck. William's brother was arrested for hiring a hit man to try to kill him and his sixth wife. Post finally died of respiratory failure in 2006 at the age of 66, leaving behind his seventh wife and nine children from his second marriage.

"After Keith Gough's wife, Louise, hit a jackpot in 2005, the family spent their wealth—as expected from undereducated nouveau riche—they bought a luxurious new home. Gough rented a $560,000 luxury box to watch his favorite soccer team, something called Aston Villa. Having quit his job at a bakery and losing purpose in life, he began drinking out of sheer boredom. Bored with him, his wife left him in 2007. He entered rehab where he met a con man who convinced Gough to join him in a series of shady business deals. This allowed the con artist to tap Gough's $1.1 million bank account. He was left with just enough money to pay the annual salaries of a gardener and a chauffeur. Even that much good life afforded by his relative wealth could not keep him healthy and alive. He died in 2010 of a heart attack, brought on by drinking and stress.

"I could list another forty, but I think I have made my point. Be careful, my friends. Choose cautiously who you trust. Watch your backs. Be loyal to each other; as you know better than anyone else, family is everything."

As it turns out, money issues are the least of the problems lying ahead for Devon, Katrina, and Ruth Carlisle.

Chapter Fifteen

September 2019

The Only True Church of Christ is in the second year of its reconstitution. Membership has declined one percent due to the scandal-mongering news media, and the financial strength of the church's corporation is twenty-one percent reduced from its zenith in 2014. 2019 has been declared a jubilee year with a worldwide church program to cry repentance, to confess all sins to the church's authorities, to double the missionary force, and to require recommitment and rebaptism. To be rebaptized, every member above the age of five years—the age of accountability—must pay a double tithe for the year and must make a public declaration of faith in Christ, then to the Council of Prophets, in close order of priority.

To kick the year off, a mass gathering takes place in Heart of Eden with over 400,000 of the faithful joining hands to make their pledge before every kind of media from throughout the United States and around the world. Because of the drama and sensationalism of the unwarranted scandal that the Antichrist Carlisle family brought on The Only True Church of Christ by their lies and by the federal government that refuses to understand the nature of the church's special marriage covenants, the generosity of the membership is brought to a fever pitch.

Three high school student bodies are present for the festivities. They are all neatly groomed and dressed in school uniforms. A sophisticated sound system is set up to make sure the world can hear the commitment from the youth. The largest student body, of course, is from the True Church Preparatory School in Eden, and the student body president and captain of the football team are selected to lead the Wyoming, Nevada, and Southern Utah students in a well-rehearsed unified statement of faith and allegiance.

The pledge is very well written and delivered in perfect unison by the assembled students. Many a tear of emotion is shed by the faithful, and the news media are almost uniformly complimentary and even enthusiastic. The week is a resounding success, not the least indicator of that success being the four million dollars that comes into the church coffers by the throngs gathered in the streets of the town. Another five million dollars comes in over the next two weeks via electronic sources.

Behind the scenes, a true test of faith is conveyed to the Council of the Prophets by the entire True Church Preparatory School football team—twenty-eight sturdy and well-disciplined young men—full of faith and jingoism. The new Prophet/President Jacob Samuel Eliasson and the six new prophets on the council gather around the conference table. The room has been thoroughly debugged and pronounced safe enough for everyone to speak freely. That search did not turn up the four remaining FBI listening devices so expertly hidden in the room. On that day, FBI listeners sitting in an electronic monitoring truck fifteen miles away record everything that is said.

"Well, my boys," Prophet/President Eliasson says with genuine warmth, "tell us what is so important to you. Let me first say how proud we all are of your full commitment. The Only True Church will live on forever and wax in strength so long as our young men are as true as you young men."

"Thank you, President," says Elmer Joseph Parker, the student body president. "Since it is Frank's idea, I'll let him explain it to you."

Frank Nichols feels awkward as he stands to speak. He is a fine athlete and a young man of action, but speech-making is daunting for him. He stammers as he begins.

"President Eliasson, the members of the football team want to do something for the cause of the church during this jubilee year. We all feel righteous wrath at the followers of Satan who have attacked The Only True Church and who mock us as they enjoy the earthly rewards stolen from Christ's own treasury. Although we believe that our Lord will burn them to a crisp as they come to face Him on Judgment Day, we have a plan for the more immediate present."

The prophet/president and the members of the Council of Prophets listen raptly as the burly footballers unfold their carefully thought out plan. The listeners in the FBI truck record every word.

FBI Special Agent Henry Weintrobe, McGee, and Ivory White arrange for Devon, Katrina, and Ruth to meet them a week later in the Camp David-Naval Support Facility Thurmont presidential retreat in Maryland, sixty miles north of Washington, to ensure absolute security. The Carlisles know better than to ask questions when McGee calls them on their burner phones. They also know it is very much in their best interests to comply with the request.

"Thank you for coming. Sorry for the cloak-and-dagger stuff, but you will understand after I tell you what has come up. Your favorite church group had a meeting a week ago where a proposal was made by what you would think was a weird source. I'll get to the details in a minute, but our FBI listeners recorded the whole meeting. The football team presented a plan to attack you guys and to annihilate all three of you in a very public demonstration of what they term, 'the awful power of God.'"

"Do they know where we live?" Ruth asks, partly angry and partly frightened.

"Apparently, they do."

"How?"

"None of us has any idea?"

"When?" asks Devon.

"I'm sorry, Devon, we could not get that. What we did get is that it is a detailed and carefully crafted plot that we should take altogether seriously. The first thing we all think you should do is to move to a new location…."

"I am not going to do that!" Katrina says passionately. "I have had enough of that. We can't run and hide forever. I think they have declared war, and we should make a stand and fight."

Weintrobe starts to interject his note of caution, but both McGee and Ivory speak up.

"I think Katrina is right. This attack will come sometime; so, why not be ready to defend against it now," McGee says.

"We can try and get them to attack someplace in the open. They apparently don't know that they are being monitored."

Ivory says, "My bet is that it will be in a public and crowded place. They have obviously been following us. We should reinstate our surveillance of each of them. We have to hit them *before* they can strike."

Weintrobe sighs. "Can't do that. We can't do anything unless they commit a crime other than to increase surveillance and security."

He goes on to communicate the details transcribed by the FBI listeners. The attack is obviously serious, and the church group apparently has the fire and manpower to carry it off. Weintrobe signs off on a doubled-up around-the-clock security detail, and McGee agrees to supplement the detail with Ivory White's "special investigations" people. Weintrobe is comfortable not knowing too many details about those people.

Chapter Sixteen

Twelve days later....

F orty-one of the richest people in the United States gather in the casual ambience of the UCLA Faculty Center on Charles Young Drive in Los Angeles for a thank-you luncheon from the university president and the faculty. To get there, the individual had to have donated in excess of $100 million over his or her lifetime to the university. All three Carlisles are latecomers to the grand donators club, and today they will become honorary members of the faculty center club. President Tucker Walsh and twenty administrators and senior faculty are seated at the head tables to welcome and honor the very generous guests.

Accommodations were made for the small army of bodyguards and security officers that the assemblage requires; not the least in number is there for the Carlisles. Devon, Katrina, and Ruth all contribute separately, and none of them request that any building or area be named for them. They travel to the UCLA campus incognito in a nondescript van driven by Ed Rainer from McGee's office, with Ivory White riding shotgun—literally. FBI agents follow unobtrusively behind, and a garish van full of Ivory's former gang friends drives ahead. That is not a bad idea, since they are the only ones who actually know the way to the rather obscure faculty center located across the street's massive parking lot 2.

The closer to the university the small convoy gets, the more edgy the security people get. Their heads swivel, and their cell phones hum as they leave the 405 Freeway and turn onto the Sunset Boulevard exit. They close ranks going east, slow down to have a wary look around, before turning right on Hilgard Avenue and then right on Westholme and into the campus. Ivory's people help the other vehicles wind their way to the large parking lot where they find themselves looking at the faculty center. Nothing appears to be out of place or suspicious; so, the entourage gets out and hurries across the street and into the building. They are early, a continuing Carlisle habit that has the advantage of allowing them to scrutinize the rest of the people as they come in.

Almost everyone is punctual; as busy people, this is just one of their appearances on that warm Los Angeles afternoon. As soon as they are seated, service begins. A large contingent of wait staff—mostly very healthy, athletic-looking young men—hurry about pushing their food carts and passing out a large shrimp cocktail on ice and a glass of freshly squeezed orange juice for everyone.

Ivory looks at the young men with his practiced suspicious eye. To him, they appear to be too clean cut for a UCLA affair— no tattoos or piercings showing. They do nothing to ratify his concerns; so, he continues his quiet watch. Two waiters deliver a large round table to the center of the dining area. It is covered with a starched new white cloth and holds an ice sculpture of the Greek Goddess Pandora—the "all-giving." She is seated by a vase, not a box, which is the correct depiction of the goddess. The waiters make a few last-minute adjustments to the striking decoration and leave. The small army of waiters once again descends upon the guests, whisking up the shrimp cocktail dishes and placing mixed greens salad plates in their place. Ivory and several of the FBI security agents do not like the rapid and almost hectic pace of the waiters; it is confusing and hard to single out any one of the young men for scrutiny.

The waiters abruptly stop as the last salad plate is placed, step back, and give a small bow. Ruth is very taken with the array of handsome and courteous young men. Ivory, Devon, and McGee not so much.

And for good reason. At a whistle from the head waiter, every man reaches under his cloth-covered food cart and pulls out a machine pistol. The security agents and Ivory and his men react almost instantly. Within two seconds, controlled pandemonium rages. Two of Ivory's gang-type security guards tackle the Carlisles, chairs and all, and throw them to the ground. Two more tip tables over the Carlisles and begin firing at the waiter-soldiers who seem heedless of their own safety. The fight moves towards the head tables that have been cleared by the university police security force. Screaming, fainting, bleeding, and dying are taking place all around. Ivory, Ed Rainer, and three FBI agents move the Carlisles back away from the melee towards the front door and safety. The FBI agents and every man and woman from McGee & Associates Investigations all have the limited focus on saving the three Carlisles whom they rightly believe are the real targets. They also rightly presume that the so-called "waiters" are cult zealots from The Only True Church of Christ and that they must think their god will ward off bullets.

Outside the faculty center, the Carlisles and their protectors make a mad dash for their vehicles. One special agent of the FBI and one of Ivory's trusted homies do not make it; but because of the swift and well-planned actions of the security force, everyone else gets out relatively unscathed.

Not so for the unfortunate guests, faculty, real wait staff, and the security forces remaining inside the building. As the Carlisle entourage moves at drag race speed to the far end of the parking lot, a powerful explosion turns the faculty center and its remaining occupants into a fireball and an eight-foot-deep smoking crater.

In the aftermath, six survivors—two of them critically burned—are found, one of whom is a "waiter"—in truth, a member of The Only True Church of Christ, and one of the captains of the Eden Heart Preparatory School football squad. Fifteen FBI agents, twenty senior UCLA administrators and faculty perish in the terroristic attack. The evidence against the church leaders in Wyoming is so overwhelming that they plead guilty and fall over themselves to turn state's evidence. The United States government, the FBI, and the people of the United States are enraged; and they do not need the media to spur them on. The church's assets are frozen; its leadership is sent to join the previous group of leaders in ignominy, despised as violators of what even cons doing hard time consider as beyond what normal humans would do. Life goes hard for the church leaders who become servants in the most demeaning possible ways to their new leaders—the alpha dogs in the prison population.

Some nobody is selected by the courts to preside over the dissolution of the church and its assets. As promised by Judge William Oxford-Randelle, the Carlisles receive the lion's share of the liquid assets and further compensation from the sale of the real property. The Carlisles are at last safe, and they are among the most generous Americans in the history of humanitarianism with their new gargantuan portfolios of wealth. The firms of Rasmussen, O'Herligy, Rodriguez, and Applewhite, and McGee & Associates are now so imperviously wealthy that both firms can pursue only cases for which they have a genuine and passionate interest.

McGee's first choice is the case that comes to be known as "The Wednesday's Child Kidnapping."

-The End-